Rescued by the Zandian

An Alien Planet Romance

Zandian Brides

Renee Rose

Rebel West

RENEE
R●SE
claimed by love

Contents

Want FREE books?   v

Prologue   1
Chapter 1   5
Chapter 2   17
Chapter 3   31
Chapter 4   45
Chapter 5   53
Chapter 6   69
Chapter 7   83
Chapter 8   93
Chapter 9   109
Chapter 10   123
Chapter 11   127
Chapter 12   135
Chapter 13   147
Chapter 14   151
Chapter 15   159
Chapter 16   163
Chapter 17   173
Chapter 18   191
Epilogue   203

Want FREE books?	207
Read all the Zandian Brides Series	209
Other Titles by Renee Rose	211
Also by Rebel West / Alexis Alvarez	217
About Renee Rose	219
About Rebel West	221
Excerpt from Conquered by the Alien Prince	223
Conquered by the Alien Prince - Sample	227

Want FREE books?

Prologue

Planet: Zandia

S*ia*

"You will answer to me from now on." The Zandian warrior who rescued me from death smiles, but there's a dominant glint in his gaze. It makes goose-bumps race across my skin.

My new master clearly enjoys control.

I've never been a pleasure slave, but something about his gaze–or perhaps it's the broad shoulders and purple skin–sends up a flare of desire.

Will he ask me to give him pleasure?

For some wild reason, I find myself hoping he will.

My body yearns for this powerful warrior in a way I've never wanted a male before. Ocretions–my previous master's species–are disgusting slobs of creatures, but this horned male is exceptional. Fierce. Beautiful.

"After all, you yourself asked for me." His horns seem to tilt in my direction.

"I did." My memories since we were beaten by the Ocretions and left to die on a defunct planet have been hazy, but this I remember. I woke wanting only him. To feel his arms around me again. The touch of his large fingers on my skin. The deep, soothing rumble of his voice. My cheeks grow warm.

"So you're mine for now. My job as your master is to protect you and help you heal. Keep you safe. Get your memory back. But also to ensure you acclimate to Zandia and accept your role here."

He arches a smooth, almost hairless brow. "You will obey me. We are lenient masters here on Zandia, and allow our humans many freedoms. However, you are still under my charge."

My belly flutters. Not from fear. From something new and different. "I understand."

"Do you?" A smile tugs at his lips—a dark and dangerous smile.

My nipples tingle. What in the stars is going on with me? I've never felt this way before. "I'll be obedient."

"You will." He chuckles, and my core clenches. "If not, Zandian masters have ways to keep our humans most compliant."

For some reason, it doesn't register as a threat. It registers as an innuendo. Teasing. Especially when he pauses and whispers into my ear. "You'll see."

The brush of his lips electrifies me. He has all of my attention now. It's almost like we are tethered with some invisible electric jumper cables.

It's almost as if he relishes the idea of punishing me.

My lips part. Inner thighs quiver. "What do you mean?" I'm melting. My body wants something I've never had. I not only like this new feeling, I crave it.

"We have unique methods to bond human to master," he murmurs. "Don't worry—most humans come to enjoy Zandian master methods as much as we do."

He brushes his knuckle down the side of my face. "But for now, let's figure out what you need to get back to full strength. Wait here."

"Not that I have a choice," I murmur. Where did that come from? I know better than to talk back to a master. But something in me wants to push his buttons. I don't even know why–maybe it has to do with that feeling his lips sparked in my core. I want more of that.

"The correct response"–he takes my chin in his hand and holds it firmly–"Is *yes, Master*."

I blink up at him. His grip is not painful in the least, but it's masterful. Firm.

"Say it, Sia. I need your obedience immediately. Now. And every time I ask."

Chapter One

One planet rotation earlier...

S*ia*

Pain explodes in my cheek.

The Ocretion guard's warted face distorts with rage as he bends down. "Idiot slave. Why didn't you tell us you weren't the pleasure gift?" Laced in with the menace is a note of panic. "Now we're missing the slaves we need. It's your fault!" His foul breath washes over me like the soft tendrils of a bloated corpse. Like I'll be, soon enough, if he doesn't stop his attack.

"Please." My voice rasps as my vision clouds. "We didn't know. I'm sorry." He picked me out of the group to be the spokesperson, and I'm suffering because I can't give him the answers he wants.

When he growls, my fear spikes. I improvise, "I'll do better!" My throat is parched, but I squeak out the words, hoping to find the magic combination of sounds to make him stop hurting us. My earlier pleas: "Slaves go where we're told," and "You ordered us onto the cargo plane, so we went," only brought punches to my face and kicks to my gut, so apologies are all I have.

"I can't understand you." His green-gray skin is mottled with boils–I can see it although my vision is narrowing, like I'm looking into a hole. He pulls his legs back, and I whimper and tuck myself into a ball, but the booted kick is to my head. "Please!" I wail, as white-hot pain flashes in my skull and sizzles down my neck to all my nerves. The implant must have loosened–he's about to–

Suddenly I know what to say, and despite the pain in my head, I scream it: "Stop! I'm Alpha Two! An Experimental! We're Alpha Two!"

The attack stops. "Cease!" The second guard's voice is taut, and there are sounds of a short scuffle. "The commander will roast us alive if we damage any of his Experimentals." And then, "Alpha Two? What's that?"

Thank stars I thought to say it. I'd laugh if I could–the assignment that's brought me nothing but pain may now save my life. Miserable though it is, I still want it.

Curses and muttered voices war with the constant wind blowing over the tall yellow grass, the sound cold and empty on the barren planet. I'm freezing, dying, while the Ocretions argue in undertones. "In trouble...Should we...get rid of them and say that... or bring them... say an attack? For now...tie them up... store them...old hut."

The words slowly cease to hold meaning. My body is hollowing out, I think, and the tortured wisp of my breath through the iron liquid in my mouth advances, until it's all I can hear. Even the wind has gone silent against my own breath.

"Please," I whisper...or think I do. At least I try. The Ocretions won't care; they have no sentiment for their human slaves beyond the stein we'll bring in a trade or the work we can do to improve abundance and utility. These particular two only care about whatever deal they're doing and saving their own careers after taking slaves they shouldn't.

Maybe I'm invoking all the near and distant universes, hoping against the odds that my cry resonates in a distant star. Or perhaps, I just want to verify that I'm still alive. But I clench my fists and send out any hopes I have, just in case it might do me any good. "Sweet Mother Earth, please."

* * *

Daven

I dive into waist-high dried grass. "Get down!" I hiss. "Take cover. They're looking this way."

Axe, my second in command, grunts, swivels, and ducks. "I thought we got away undetected after retrieving the recording device." His voice is so low I barely hear it.

"I did too, but they're checking their perimeter." I peer towards the Ocretion encampment.

My eyes have already adjusted to the inky night on Simak 14–a supposedly uninhabited foreign planet–using only starlight to see. The night vision on my eyepiece enhances the view.

A quarter-click from us, several stumpy Ocretions walk around in widening circles, holding light bars. And weapons. For us?

It's a strange miracle of fate that we found their ship here in the first place–after we saw them unmask and land, we couldn't resist the opportunity to spy, since we have a completely cloaked ship that could land without their notice. It's not every planet rotation that we Zandians get a front row seat to see what the Ocretions are planning, and lately this kind of intel is more critical than ever before.

The sight of their warty, stinking bodies irritates me.

Ocretions--the largest and most powerful species in the galaxy--offered our prince shelter after the Finn took our planet, but now that we've won it back and are working on repopulation, relations have become strained.

I whisper while I stare. "I don't know why the Ocretions are meeting here with Karran tech craftsmen." The Karran are tall, and their large translucent eyes gleam like neon in my night vision scope. They stand back behind the Ocs.

"Odd. They don't usually do business together." Axe puts a hand to his laser gun. "We need to avoid a fight."

"I know. Stay low. I don't think they see us."

From here, we can't hear the Ocretions' conversation, but their bodies are tense. Alert. The Karran—I note that they aren't carrying weapons—look jumpy, their long necks bending and ducking.

The group of them have a small encampment set up, and behind that, their aircraft, four big Oc carriers, and two smaller Karran transport ships. Uncloaked. Clearly, they did not expect visitors.

"We need to get back to our ship. Get the *veck* out of here and back to Zandia."

About a quarter-mile away, there's a run-down shanty of a building. It stands alone in this vast expanse of dried brush and desiccated grasses.

I nod at the distant shack. "It's not on the direct path to our ship, but if we hide out there for a while, we can be sure no being is following us."

"Agree." Axe nods. "On your mark."

"Go." We get to our feet and race to the building, my lungs burning in the thinner atmosphere.

No shots sizzle past our skin or into our disguised bodies, thank *veck*, and in seconds we're behind the structure, panting, peering around the sides of it, guns up. Watching–just in case.

I force myself to quiet my breathing, so I can hear.

There's no sound at all beyond the constant low howl of the wind that sets the grass stirring constantly. This planet, although the atmosphere is a close enough match for our bodies, seems to be utterly vacant. Except, of course, for the Ocretions who nearly found us spying outside their encampment, taking long-range vid.

"This planet is supposed to be uninhabited," Axe observes. "And untouched. By intergalactic treaty."

I scoff. "No being honors those treaties. Anyway, an abandoned planet is a perfect place for the Ocretions to set up a secret way station for illegal trade storage."

"That's just the thing." Axe's voice is cautious. "If this is a trading stop, it's a piss poor one. Just this one little hut? An ancient one, at that? They didn't build this–it's leftover from ages ago."

"Maybe the holo recording of them will give us more information." I touch the satchel again. "We'll analyze it back on Zandia. The audio picked up more than our ears could hear."

"Let's hope it's good info." Axe's voice is low.

"On my count, run to our ship."

He nods.

"One, two –"

A sudden noise inside the shack stops me. We both leap to attention.

"What the *veck* was that?" Axe asks.

"Help, please." It's a weak voice, speaking Ocretion. Sounds female. Young. "Please. Help me."

Axe frowns and looks at me. "We can't help her. If we do, the Ocretions will know that someone has been here.

That will make them suspicious. We need to think of the mission."

The voice is raspy and desperate. "I'm dying. Please. I don't understand you, but I heard the word *Zandia*. Are you Zandians? Please help me."

"She sounds human."

Axe and I look at each other, and his frown increases. He dislikes humans. "*Veck*," he mutters.

I purse my lips. "Change of plans. We take her, no matter her species. If she's been with the Ocretions, she'll have additional intel on their plans that could be invaluable."

Axe considers this with a deeper frown. "True."

"If we leave her, she could *veck* up our mission with one word. If she lives and tells the Ocretions she heard Zandians talking outside the hut? The Ocs might take off, and whatever we learned here will be useless. You know they're skittish--and with our strained relations, we can't risk aggravating them by spying."

"*Veck* me twice," Axe growls. "This isn't how this was supposed to go."

"We weren't even cleared to land here by Master Seke." My voice is wry mentioning our commander and master at arms. "He said it was too dangerous. Maybe this human will give us enough info, along with the holo, to make this worthwhile."

I'm not actually worried about what Master Seke will do; he trusts us, after all. Because we desperately need to know what the Ocs are planning. The humans on our planet are at risk.

I test the door of the shack--it opens easily, no locks. We check for traps or tricks, but it seems there are none--just a tiny form lying in the corner, breathing with difficulty.

Even in the dim light, I can see that I was right: she is a human.

She's dirty, her thin caftan ripped and stained, revealing a supple body tied with ropes so tight that they're cutting off her circulation. The skin around her lips is cracked and broken. Her head bears an injury; there's a huge bruise and dried blood on her forehead and the top of her skull–was she hit with something? Kicked with a boot? It doesn't look good. I try to assess the damage, ignoring the reaction my body has to her. Underneath the dirt and damage, it's plain she's beautiful. Stunning, really.

"Need...fluid." Her eyelids flutter.

I bend down and lean close to her face. I speak in Ocretion. "We're here to help."

"Please." She doesn't seem to understand, even though I spoke her language. Humans have been enslaved by the Ocretions for over two thousand years.

Zandia's strained relations with Ocretia stem from the fact that we've learned the species we are most compatible to breed with is human. On the surface, this seems like a non-problem. They own slaves--we buy them to breed.

Except it hasn't worked that way. Our prince--now king--fell in love with his human breeder. In fact, every Zandian who's taken a human to breed has fallen in love. Their species changes us. They bond strongly to us, and our need to care for and protect them brings out emotions that Zandian warriors didn't used to have.

And so the Ocretions and their galactic laws forbidding human freedom have come to grate upon us. Tensions between our two species are mounting as word travels through the galaxy that we allow humans a great deal of free will on our planet.

"Who are you? Why did they leave you here like this?"

I touch her cheek. I'm enraged that any being could leave a human in such a state. It's cruel beyond belief.

She blinks but doesn't speak. Her gaze looks wild.

It stinks in here, far worse than her one body. I look around again, but the small space holds nothing else. "We'll get you fluid soon. Just hold on."

Something akin to panic wells in me. *Veck*, why don't I have something to help her immediately?

"Said they were going to maybe kill us..." she blinks and winces, tilts her head in question, as if she can't focus on her own thoughts. Maybe she can't, abused as she is. "All of us..." she trails off, voice confused. Her energy flags.

"Us?" I narrow my eyes. She's alone.

She gasps. Shudders.

I look more closely at her face and delicate body. She has long, thick wavy black hair and light brown skin. Healthy, she'd command a huge price at auction. The Ocretions don't treat humans well, but this is beyond even their typical greedy behavior–they like their slave bounty to be in top shape to sell for the best prices in the galaxy.

"We might not make it." Her eyes shut and don't open.

"Why would they leave her here like this?" I scowl. I want to pound my fists into the faces of her former masters.

Axe shrugs. "I don't get it either. But I guess she's ours, now." His voice has far less enthusiasm than a Zandian would usually have at finding a human female. But then, he was with me when we were betrayed by one.

I barely stop a low growl from rumbling in my throat. *She's mine. Not ours.*

But that's not the way things work on Zandia. We have so few Zandian females left that our species has exploited the compatibility of human females with our males to repopulate our planet. Many Zandians have mated in multiples--two, three, or even four males to one human female. But for some inexplicable reason, I want this female. And I want her all to myself.

He adds, "She can be bred by Zandians, for sure. But it's a *vecking* inconvenient time to run across one and steal her."

"*Save* her," I correct. And she's definitely worth saving.

I sniff again; the fetid air is surely not helping the human breathe. "Let's get out of here."

I glance at the human. She's still breathing although it's shallow. Her hair is lank and greasy, her body broken, and I feel an urgent, unfamiliar feeling to protect her. Save her.

"Hurry." But as I step forward, something creaks under my foot. I look down and catch sight of an outline.

"There's a trap door here in the floor," I whisper to Axe, pointing down.

He grunts.

"Dangerous, but worse to leave it unexplored."

He nods. I gesture; he pulls up the door slowly, and I point my laser gun down as I look into the hole. I risk using my lightstick on low setting to get a better view. "It's like a crawl space hewn into the rock and dirt. And is that?"

"*Veck* the stars, what is that?" Axe gags at the odor that pours from the opening. It's the stench of death. My human coughs and moans.

The shallow, dusty hole beneath the shack is stuffed with bound bodies, all females, and there's no room for more. At least five or six.

The two of us drop into the space immediately; there's no ladder down, but it's not needed with such a small area. I recognize the willowy form of a Za'ir, prized at auctions. I check her pulse. "Dead." I check another one, a shorter

Za'ir. "Also dead. They let their slaves die." My blood boils as I enhance the light, making it brighter.

"This one's alive." Axe picks up a human female. "You take her."

I climb back up and reach down, accepting the small body as he hands her to me.

I'm irrationally relieved that there's a second human, so I won't have to share mine with Axe, not that he's even asked that of me. Not that he has ever shown interest in taking one because he dislikes humans for some reason he's never shared.

I study her as I shift her in my arms. She doesn't produce the same possessive sentiments the first one did. The same sense of destiny.

Zandians don't believe in fate. Before we mated with humans, we didn't speak much of love. My attraction to the first slave must be chemical. Our genes are most compatible for mating.

That must be it.

I deposit the second slave carefully on the ground. When I turn back, Axe has hoisted up two more human females and is untying them, so they can walk. "All the Za'ir are dead. These human females need fluid immediately." None of the others are beaten like my human—yes, I've already decided she's mine and mine alone—but they're not in good shape.

I assist the weakened females, gently rubbing their wrists to help circulation. "Who are you?" I ask. "What happened?"

They're stunned, eyes wide, in shock. None of them seem able to speak; they can barely stand. I give up on talking; there's no time anyway. We'll get the information later.

When we're all out, I curse again. "*Vecking* monsters."

I stare down at my female. She's lovely--too slender, but softened with round breasts and dark nipples that beg to be sucked. I scoop her up--she's so light in my arms, like nothing.

"Let's get the *veck* out of here," I order. I should throw her over my shoulder and take a second one on the other side, but I'm not willing to hold her in any way but this. She's too delicate. Or maybe, I just can't look away from those lovely dark eyes. I have no business claiming her, but I want to. *Veck*, do I want to. I'm drawn to this one, mesmerized by her.

Axe picks up the second female--one with her head shaved and punishment tattoos across one shoulder and down her arm.

The other three seem able to walk, after he speaks to them in a low voice and points, gives them a nudge to get them into motion. We exit the shack in a ragged line, and Axe closes the door behind us, leaving it the way we found it. We start to walk to the craft, but that's too slow. Eventually, Axe takes two females in his arms and races them to the ship, then comes back for more, while I carry my wounded human alone, moving carefully, so I don't break her before it's too late to save her.

She sighs and nestles into me as we move, and something stirs in my chest--but there's no time to think about it.

It's seconds before we're at our cloaked craft. "Karl, start us up in stealth mode," I bark at the warrior I left to protect the craft.

Axe's lip curls in disdain as he holds a fluid tube to a human's lips. I do the same for my female, then get fluid tubes to the other three. As I do, Axe checks the vitals of my female. "She's in bad shape," he mutters. "She might not make it."

My stomach drops. I've only seen her for a short time, but something about her makes me feel protective. "Do everything you can, Axe. We need to save her--them."

I get blankets for the females and drape them around their shoulders. They sit silent, all of them trembling.

"We're getting you out," I tell them, not knowing if they even comprehend anything. "You're safe here. We have a doctor who will heal you."

Karl starts the engines in silent mode, and the craft lifts, a marvel of technology. There is no action from the Ocretion crafts parked near their camp: Our cloaking is still better than their surveillance. They're the second-best in the galaxy. We're number one. A small planet, but a brilliant one.

As we leap into hyperdrive, I maneuver around asteroids and put the craft into autopilot. Then I step over to examine our new bounty. All I can focus on is the one I saved in my arms.

The little human with long lashes and beautiful dark eyes.

Mine now, for better or worse.

Chapter Two

Outer Space

S *ia*
Through the haze of pain, I sense movement above me.

Instinctively I try to huddle into a ball. "No," I whimper. "Don't hurt me again."

My limbs quiver in terror. The Ocretions are back, and this time, I don't know what will happen. Somehow I saved us before–what was it I said? The thoughts skitter around inside my skulls like hail in a storm, then splinter into confetti. I can't remember anything.

"No being is going to hurt you. You're safe now." A low voice, deep and pleasant, at least compared with the Ocretian grunts, rolls over me. And there's a fluid tube in my mouth. I suck greedily, even though my mouth is on fire, and the broken skin burns.

"We rescued you. You're on our ship. We're going to help you."

I can't seem to open my eyes. My hands--somehow untied?--flutter up to touch them.

"Shh, don't do that. We put on bandages. Your corneas were dried and scratchy. We've put on healing salve."

"Please. Take it off." My terror mounts.

"It should be all right if you take it off." The male speaking to me seems to be conversing with another. "That salve works quickly."

"If she sees us, maybe she'll relax." The second male seems to agree.

Gentle hands remove something from my head.

"Slowly," a voice cautions.

I blink, and everything is blurry.

"Here." He wipes at my eyes with a soft cloth. "Try again."

I blink, and he zooms into focus. He is very tall, with broad shoulders. He has purple skin and horns atop his smooth head. It's the same voice I heard before, but back in the shack, I couldn't focus. I see now that he's a Zandian warrior. His face is full of angles and planes, and for some reason, I think he's handsome--although that makes no difference at this moment.

"I'm Daven." The handsome one observes me then gestures to another Zandian, who's a little shorter and stock-ier. "This is Axe. We rescued you and some other females from an isolated planet in an old trader's hut."

Thank the stars. I cough. My whole body hurts. I can barely make out where I am. I'm lying on something soft, at least, and there are bright lights all around. "You saved me?" I look up at him. "Saved us?" My eyes fill with tears.

"Yes, all of the humans were still alive. And you're with me now. I swear no being will ever hurt you again." He growls it then touches my arm. Pulls his hand back like he shouldn't be touching me although I don't mind. His hand is warm, and I crave his touch. More than anything, I want him to hold me. Although that's a strange thought. I've never desired to be touched by another species before—especially not a male.

The other Zandian frowns. "Be careful. They can't be trusted."

"She's injured," Daven growls.

"And you're too trusting of human females. Remember what happened last time you chose a mate," he reminds Daven, sending me a cold look before looking away.

For some reason, I hate the idea that Daven has had a mate.

Daven frowns but doesn't answer. He turns back to me.

I take a breath. Everything hurts, and I whimper.

"What happened to you?" Daven leans down, touches my face, then pulls his hand back when I wince. "Why were you tied up there?"

"They were going to trade us," I remember aloud. "But they discovered we're not pleasure slaves, so they were beating me. Trying to find out how the mistake happened. I think they were going to kill me. But then I told them— I'm..." I trail off. "I know about..." Something in my head whirs, and there's a terrible pain.

This time, memories are there, but I cannot divulge them. It's been hammered into me since I became an Experimental: Those who talk about the work of Alpha 2 die. I've seen it firsthand.

"About what?" urges the closer Zandian. "You know about what?" The two of them flash a look at each other then focus on me. "This is important."

"About Al-" I want to tell them, but my whole body rebels. Images of the punishments, the tests, come flooding back. The work itself, what it's planned for, my friends, back on the original planet, still enslaved, doing the work. I stammer out, "The other slaves" just because the Zandians are staring at me, and I need to say something.

"The other slaves?" Daven frowns. "What about them? Tell us." His voice is commanding, but it doesn't scare me. He doesn't sound cruel, more like a being who is accustomed to leading.

My head starts to ache, and images flash rapid-fire through my mind. The thoughts break apart again. "I can't think." The floor tilts, and I'm falling to the side...or things are rolling around inside my skull. That's it, isn't it? Something inside my skull? A thought emerges, but I can't quite follow the trail. "There's something wrong with my brain." I attempt to slow myself down. The more I chase the thought, the more my body responds with panic.

"*Veck*, the head injury. We need to stabilize her, so Dr. Daneth can help."

Sounds and images become one big amalgamation of sensation. I gasp as I fall into a void. "Help!" I cry. "I'm falling!"

"She's crashing. Better put her under until we arrive."

There's a prick as a needle slides into my arm and then-- oblivion.

* * *

Planet: Zandia

Daven

I didn't want to leave my little human, not even with Dr. Daneth, the galaxy's best scientist. But, of course, I had to.

Now we're in the war room with the King and his council to report. A giant oval table hovers in the center of the room, and the king's advisors sit around it. Axe and I stand to report.

"Play it again." Our master-at-arms and my commander, Seke, leans forward, face intent.

"Of course." I tap the holo device and glance at the Zandians seated around the table in the royal meeting quarters: Master Seke, my second-in-command, Axe, and none other than King Zander himself. The king's face holds concern. The rumors and chatter about a new and more powerful Ocretian attack have been escalating.

On the device, grainy figures move on the screen. It's the recording I made of the Ocretions and the Karran back on the forlorn planet where we found the humans.

"Going to need..." the audio cuts out *"at least 1,000 linear hects of the compound." The Oc in charge crosses his stubby arms and looks at the K sitting beside him. "If that goes well, we may have another, more lucrative task for you."*

"And just a start. We'll also want you to run a ..." the sound quality fizzles out.

"Forgive me, my lord." I fiddle with the controls, trying to get better audio. "No matter how we enhance, I can't understand what he said."

The king holds up a finger. The holo continues.

"And as for the price?" The Karran looks at his companion. "You agree?"

"The stein is not a problem." The Ocretion waves his warted hand. "But the pleasure slaves we will deliver another time. The batch we brought was..." he wrinkles his nose. "Substandard."

I'm satisfied to hear this tracks with what the little

human told me. A slave mix-up happened, and she and her friends were left to die.

"*That is a shame. We were looking forward to the best pleasure in the galaxy.*" The Karran scowls.

"*The wrong batch was loaded onto the cargo. Workers, unskilled in what you desire. They would have been nothing but a nuisance. We'll give you double—delivered wherever you want.*"

The Karran look at each other and nod. "Acceptable."

"*We need the materials as soon as possible.*" The Ocretion frowns.

"*With that much, you will have enough to...*" The Karran raises his eyebrows, clearly curious.

"*It's not your business.*" The Ocretion's voice is curt, threatening. "*We're paying you to supply, not to conjecture. Or to talk.*" He puts a hand on his weapon. "*You are not a target to us...as long as our trade relationship is intact.*" He raises an eyebrow. "*And secret.*"

"*Understood.*" The Karran raises both wavy arms. "*Our silence is absolute.*"

"*Good.*"

The holo flickers off, and we sit in silence for a second or two.

I tap the device. "They don't say what compound they want. It could be something needed to make a new weapon or something for chemical warfare."

The king nods. "If not an attack, perhaps they're stockpiling a massive amount of firepower, so they can easily come in and force a planet to surrender to their demands."

Master Seke furrows his brow. "What they like to call a *beneficial assistive takeover*. If they come here to Zandia, they'd probably wish to control us and take away our human females."

We fall silent for a moment, faces somber.

Erick, one of the advisors says, "They've been making a lot of noise lately about how we've negated any goodwill they provided by taking humans and providing them sanctuary. Say it's causing tension in the galaxy and causing them issues. I think they may definitely be planning something—involving our planet."

The king's voice is taut. "We need more details about what they're creating. What do we know about the Karran? What can they supply for the Ocretions?"

"I don't know. We have our best scouts on it." Seke says.

"I'm assuming some manner of explosive or airborne chemical agent," I say. "And even more concerning is what they want to be engineered. Some kind of long-range delivery system?" I shake my head. "We just don't know. And that makes us weak."

Axe clears his throat. "Can we eliminate the Karrans or disrupt the trade?"

"Look into it. But at this point, our best option is to find out more—exactly what they're doing—so we can counter it with weapons and systems of our own." The King stands. "This is critical for Zandia. We need to prepare for them." He looks at the team. "What of the humans who were recovered? Do they have information?" He taps his comms unit, and Dr. Daneth's holo springs up.

He bows. "My lord." He nods to the rest of us.

"Do the humans have information on what the Ocretions are planning?"

The doctor purses his lips. "The ones in better condition are coming out of shock but haven't said anything useful yet. They don't know anything, at least not more than anecdotally, about military or operations. My vital recorder tells me that they're being about eighty-five percent truthful. I think it would benefit us to assign masters to each one to help extract their memories...and the truth about what they know."

The king considers this.

Dr. Daneth adds, "They tell us Sia, the more injured one, is some kind of tech worker. She's the one who will have the best intel. She seems to be their *de facto* leader."

"And how is Sia?" My voice is tight. I think of the delicate human I held in my arms, the one I can't get out of my mind, even as we discuss military operations. If masters are assigned to the females, I need to be hers.

I want to master her in every way. Make her learn to do my bidding. To obey. I want to reward her for her compliance and show her pleasure through punishment and praise. This is how Zandians assimilate humans onto our planet. We bond them to us through sexual mastery.

The doctor taps his wristband and looks up. "Stable. She was severely dehydrated, and her electrolytes were abnormal. If you hadn't rescued her when you did, she probably would have died. The odd thing..." he trails off.

"Yes?" I lean forward, almost snapping.

"Two things, actually. The current head wound looked terrible, but it was more bruising and dried blood than anything. Her dry eyes and body bruises have healed, as has the broken rib. But she has healed scars on her head that would indicate recent brain surgery. So do all of the humans you brought in."

"Elaborate." The king's voice is even. "Did you find evidence of any changes to their brains?"

"I've done scans, and there's no indication of anything foreign inside their heads, no chips or plates or enhancements. No transmissions. But the scars match on all of them, and it's troubling. The Ocretions did something, or tried, at least."

"When they are capable of communicating, surely they will tell us."

Beside me, I sense Axe shift and hear his almost inaudible scoff.

"They'll do what they can to help." Perhaps I'm trying to convince myself. But when I think of my human, I already feel protective. Surely I wouldn't feel that for a creature who wasn't good for our planet?

The doctor looks at the king then back at me. "I hope so. But my initial assessment is that Sia is hiding something. In addition, the current head wound itself should not have caused such deep agitation and memory loss. She's also experiencing severe anxiety. Right now, she's not capable of even conversing without going into a panic attack. I suspect she's afraid to speak freely."

"How should we treat her?" If she's going to be mine, I need to know how to help her.

Dr. Daneth taps his tablet again, examining some numbers, then looks up. "Vitals are better. I suggest we do our best to comfort her and help her feel safe, and as she heals, hopefully, she'll be able to tell us more. Especially about whatever it is she feels she has to hide." He looks at me. "Daven."

"Yes?" My heart thuds thinking of the little human how fragile she is. How lovely, even though battered. It hurts me to think that she's almost beyond repair.

"She asked for you."

Because she's mine. I hardly understand the emotion that floods me. Possessiveness. Need.

But Axe was right. I have to be careful. I rescued a

human once before and wished to mate her, only to have her betray us the first moment she could.

I stand taller. "By name?"

"No."

I ignore the stab of disappointment.

"She was babbling, then she mentioned" –he clears his throat– *"The handsome one who carried me.* From the report, I know that was you."

My horns thicken.

The human thinks I'm handsome.

There's subdued chuckling from around the table.

The king frowns, and everyone goes silent.

Dr. Daneth continues, "I suspect she already partially bonded from the rescue." He glances at King Zander. "I recommend she be remanded to Daven's custody for further questioning and integration."

"Daven." King Zander looks at me. "If she remembers you, then that's a start. For now, you will be her master and protector here on Zandia while she heals. Bond her to you. Spend time with her, talk to her. Do everything and anything in your power to get information from her, no matter how slight. Whatever it takes. Anything could help. We know she must have something in her head that can help us. If she doesn't take to you, we'll find another. But give it your best."

I bow as inwardly I glory at the assignment. "Yes, my lord."

"And good work on getting this holo. We know at least that they're planning something big–and potentially deadly. And soon."

"Thank you, my lord. We will continue to do everything we can to learn more. We have scanners checking intergalactic chatter, we're doing recon missions, and we're reaching out to any known allies. We won't leave anything undone."

"Good. You two are dismissed. Get back to work."

Axe and I bow.

"My lord?" Axe says, hesitating after he straightens.

King Zander lifts a questioning brow.

"What about the other rescues?"

King Zander studies Axe for a moment. "Did you bond with one of them?"

"No," Axe snaps, too quickly. "I just–" he shakes his head. "They should be closely watched, that's all. We don't know if they can be trusted."

The king considers him without comment.

"Of course, you know that. Forgive me, my lord," Axe says quickly, realizing he's overstepped.

"I will assign a Zandian master to each rescued human. If you wish to be considered for the job, or for a particular human, now is the time to speak."

I expect Axe to deny it–I know how much he mistrusts humans, but he scrubs a hand across his jaw. "One of them will need closer watch than the others. She's clearly caused her previous masters grief, based on her shorn hair and punishment ink."

"I will take that into consideration," King Zander says. "We need to pump each of them for any information they have. Even a little snippet of info they think is insignificant might help us." He pauses. "Dr. Daneth, please give me your recommendations for assignments as the humans are ready to leave your care."

The doctor nods. "Yes, my lord."

King Zander dismisses us a second time. "Then get to work."

Axe and I bow once more and walk out together. "Don't trust that human," he warns.

I stiffen my jaw. "She's on our planet under my watch. She can't do any harm."

He glowers. "You don't know that."

I square my shoulders. "Hopefully she has more intel she can share with us. She could be a great contribution to Zandia."

Axe looks at me with doubt etched on his features.

I want to punch his face in but only because I know he's right. My judgment when it comes to females can't be trusted.

I nearly got us all killed by believing one last time.

"What she said on the ship–she does know something," Axe says. "It's critical that you find it out."

"I will," I pledge–not just to him, but to myself. To my king. To my planet.

"If she finds you attractive, she'll surely bond to you with proper training and punishment. You can use that."

I hate him even talking about her. "I'll do what I need to do."

"Just don't mate her. Not until you know she can be trusted."

"Of course not." I step to the side. "I'm going to the med bay right now to see if she'll talk to me."

"Don't mate her," he repeats. Then he looks toward the med bay with a scowl. "I'll go, too. To make sure Flora isn't a threat to Zandia."

Interesting. Flora is the human he referred to–the one with the tattoos, shorned head. Axe may not trust humans, but something tells me he's interested, just the same.

"Perhaps I could be of assistance in questioning her. We all need to do what we can."

"Right." It's obvious what he's saying, and it has nothing to do with intel. "If you want to be assigned as her master, you should have requested it."

"I don't," he snaps. "I'm just concerned, that's all."

Right. *Concerned.*

"Fine. Let's go see them."

As I walk toward the building, my body vibrates with anticipation. When I'm on task, I always work at one hundred percent capacity, ready to do my best for my fellow Zandians. But this is something else. This is something... physical. Yet also more. Seeing the little human again creates a tidal wave of sensations in my body.

I can't wait to see what happens after I've fully claimed her as my own.

Not as a mate–not until I can trust her–but her body belongs to me now, and I can't wait to use it.

Chapter Three

S*ia*

Panic frays my nerves, making my headache return, despite the meds the Zandian doctor gave me. Not remembering who I am or where I came from makes everything worse.

I recognized the human females I was brought in with, but how I know them is unclear. We were slaves together, obviously. But I remember nothing of the planet where they picked us up. Nor how we got there. Nor what happened before that.

And while they should be a comfort to me, instead I crave the presence of the warrior who rescued me.

I don't know why, but I have some sense that he will clear everything up for me.

Which is irrational because I don't think I knew him before the last planet rotation.

He comes into the clinic where I've been held since we landed, and my pulse picks up speed.

I slide off the examination table. "Master," I say, then stop in confusion. "I'm sorry, you're not my master, are you?" Then I'm befuddled again. Why did I even think that?

The warrior's lips twitch, his horns thicken and lean in my direction. "Would you like me to be your master?" His voice is a low, deep rumble. I can't decide if there's a trace of sexual suggestiveness in it.

I can't decide if I want there to be.

"Yes," I answer honestly.

Again, it's irrational, but this male's quiet authority grounds me where every other being here makes me nervous. I don't know what's happening, but I want him to be the one I answer to. The one who commands me. He feels safe.

He walks up to me, places his large hands around my waist and lifts me easily back up on the table. "Did you have permission to get down?" There's a trace of sternness to his tone, but for some reason, it feels teasing.

But masters don't tease, do they? I wrack my brain, trying to remember my last master. For some reason, even thinking about him frightens me.

Heat flushes across my skin--I can't tell if it's because I'm ashamed of being scolded or because his large hands still rest at my waist, their gentle weight warming my skin through the thin medical gown. "I-I'm not sure. Do I?"

His lips twitch. "I'll find out." He turns to the physician, keeping one hand lightly resting on me. "Doctor Daneth? Is Sia required to stay here?"

I'm absurdly pleased to hear my name from his lips. Like I belong to him. He's the familiar thing in a place where everything is new and different.

The doctor, who I found to be cool and professional but not unkind turns. "I am finished with her for now. You may bring her to the holding bay where they are keeping the slaves she came in with. Then come speak to me about her placement."

The warrior bows to the doctor, who must be his superior and turns back to me. He picks me up by the waist and lowers me to my feet as if I weigh nothing. When my knees buckle, he catches my elbow to steady me.

"Can you walk, little human?"

"Yes, Master," I murmur.

The warrior makes a sound like, "Hmm" or "Mm." He sounds satisfied. His large hand stays on my elbow as he guides me out of the clinic and into a long white corridor. The building is beautiful--tremendously different from Ocretion structures. At least that's my first thought, but when I try to remember previous buildings, I only get a foggy image of some kind of laboratory. As soon as I try to chase the memory, though, everything goes blank.

Still, I'm certain I've never seen such immense wealth and opulence. The corridor floor is made of gleaming marble or some other stone. The walls are polished plaster with pale colors woven right into the texture, not painted over the top.

There's a lightness to this planet I haven't experienced before.

Then again, it may be the drugs they gave me for my head injury.

I draw in several deep breaths. I need to clear this headache, so I can understand what exactly is going on.

"Is this your space?" He gestures to the small but comfortable alcove. The other rescues are down the hall in similar quarters. We're locked in, but it doesn't feel like any jail I've ever seen or imagined.

"Yes." My head spins again, and I sway.

He grabs me and lowers me to a soft sleeping platform. "Here, sit."

I blink at him as he wraps a soft blanket around my shoulders. His fingers graze my skin, halfway between accidental and deliberate, and I shudder. They've given me a soft gown with short sleeves, far more comfortable than any clothing I've worn before. I like feeling his fingers on my arm.

"Are you cold?" His voice is low, and again, teasing.

"Ah—no." In fact, I feel warm all over, and tingly, especially where he touched me.

"Good." He observes me. He doesn't touch me again, though, and a flicker of disappointment rushes through my body.

I stare at his handsome face, trying to figure him out. Make sense of all this.

"So you rescued me?" I know he did, but I need to say it out loud to make it fall into place. Try to unlock the parts of my brain that are inaccessible.

"You were lying, near dead, in an abandoned hut on a supposedly abandoned planet. Left there by Ocretions, we think. And you all have matching head scars."

"But why?" My voice cracks. I reach up to touch my head and find the oddly familiar ridge under my hairline. I run my index finger along it. "What is this?"

"That's what we're hoping you can tell us." His voice is somber. "It's critical for our planet and for every being who lives here. Zandians and humans alike."

I contemplate this. "My name is Sia. I know that much."

He touches my hand then takes it into his. The spark of feeling that courses through me is a shock and a surprise. I like his touch more than anything.

"I'm a lab worker." I say it without knowing what it

means, and then the information presents itself in my mind in oddly perfect little video clips, as if I'm watching a holo. Is this how memory is supposed to work?

"I organize glassware and run basic experiments with chemicals, but I'm not a chemist. I'm just a basic worker." It's amazing how the knowledge is coming back in, like water filling a cup. "I can see it!" I look at him, anxiety welling up, but his eyes calm me.

"Keep going." Daven squeezes my hand. "Everything you remember, just tell me."

I nod. " My master's name is -"–it comes to me–"Torok. But we don't–he's not a master the way you are. He never touches us. My face feels hot. "We're not pleasure slaves."

I don't know why I mentioned pleasure. Daven hasn't insinuated he will be using me that way. Yet when I say it, his horns lengthen and lean in my direction, as if he's interested.

Stars, for some reason, I very much want him to be interested.

I clear my throat and go on. "We live in dorms and report for work. It's highly regulated. We don't walk anywhere without guards. We eat a special diet. Because we're experimentals."

Suddenly my head buzzes. I'm not supposed to say that, about being experimental. I touch my skull, the strange scar that I don't understand or remember. The buzzing intensifies, and I recall an Ocretion face, one of my master's main tech leaders: *You must never talk about the work of Project Alpha, or you can be eliminated. Is that clear?*

"I can't–" Images flash into my mind in a split second. *I see a leering Ocretion face above me. Then an image of an operating room, sterile instruments and white walls. A needle coming toward my head.*

I cry out.

"Easy, easy." Daven's arms are around me, and the images are gone.

"What hurts? Your head?"

"Yes." I find I'm sweating. My breath comes in pants.

"Did you remember something?" He sounds urgent.

"Um...yes, I think so."

"What did you remember?" His arms tighten. "Tell me. It's very important, Sia."

"I'm sorry. I–I can't remember much. A needle. And a face?" And now the images are gone entirely. How can that be? How could I just forget so fast? "But...now I'm not sure. It's just gone!"

He looks into my eyes. "I see." His face registers disappointment, I think. But also understanding. He believes me.

But even as I say this, another flash lights up my mind. This one is different, more powerful somehow. Like it means something to me on a very personal level.

"We have to keep the secret or we all die. You know this, Sia." My friend Flora looks up at me with fierce determination, her eyes huge in her newly shorn head. Her scars are fresh and red, raised and thick like bloated veins.

I wince as I take her hand, and agree with her. "We will never say a word to any being if we manage to escape, even ones who seem trustworthy. They would kill us in a heartbeat if they knew the truth about us, even the supposedly nice ones. Because what's inside our heads means no being can ever trust us."

The flashback stops, but this time I remember it, and the human I was with–Flora. She's here, too, on Zandia. What in Mother Earth happened to us?

I blink and look away. I want to trust my new master, but something about this memory confirms some other loyalty–and until I figure this out, I need to keep quiet. I know this in my gut.

"Did you remember something else?" His voice is even.

"No." I shake my head. Still, I don't look at him. "Just tired. My head aches, and I can't think properly. It's scary." That last part is true. But can he tell I'm leaving something out?

"It's going to be all right." His voice is strong and even, and for some reason, I want to believe him. Even if everything is supremely wrong at the moment.

"Who are you exactly?" It's easier than asking, "Who am I?" Because despite what I remember so far, I clearly know very little about myself or my history.

"I'm Daven. A Zandian warrior. Your new master."

"Okay." I nod.

"You're on Zandia. You're safe here. We're not going to hurt you. We revere our humans."

"Okay." This does not begin to sum up the supreme relief I feel at his words, but it's all I can manage at this point.

"I'm so grateful you saved us." Again, I try to summon my memories to see what I can recall beyond the very few things I've told him.

Panic starts to well up. "I can't!" No more images come. My past is such a blank. I'm empty.

He takes my face gently between his strong hands. "Stop. Breathe. In and out."

Immobilized, all I can do is gaze into his eyes, deep and mesmerizing.

"Like this."

He puts a hand on my chest, and although it's not a sexual touch, little flickers of arousal flutter in my belly, even as the anxiety starts to fade. "Deep breaths. Don't think about anything. Just breathe with me."

I stare into his eyes and breathe in and out until the panic eases, and I can stand existence again.

"It's going to come back, your memory. It always does."

"You seem so certain." I tug at the blanket, pulling a soft strand between two fingers.

"It's been our experience." He shrugs. "Every human who comes here eventually gets better."

I like the implication of his words—that they care here about humans. "Every human? How many are here?" Even though I can't remember much about myself, I know humans are chattel to the universe. And I know I've been mistreated badly. It sounds like this planet is a refuge of some kind to humans, and If there are many of us here, on this planet, what a blessing!

He regards me. "More than you might imagine." He continues, "And about your master. It's all right if you don't remember much about your old one yet. Because now I'm your master, little human, here on Zandia."

* * *

Daven

Sia's breath catches, but it doesn't appear to be with fear. No, I believe she's attracted to me. She likes the idea of having me as her master.

"You will answer to me from now on." My horns thicken at the thought of how I will keep the little human in line. The methods I will employ to exact good behavior. "After all, you yourself asked for me."

"I did," she murmurs softly, her face flushing.

"So you're mine for now. My job as your master is to

protect you and help you heal. Keep you safe. Get your memory back. But also to ensure you acclimate to Zandia and accept your role here."

I arch a brow. "You will obey me. We are lenient masters here on Zandia and allow our humans many freedoms. However, you are still under my charge."

Her berry lips part. "I understand."

"Do you?"

Is it wrong that I hope she tests me? That I can't wait to give her a little taste of my punishment?

"I'll be obedient," she promises.

Veck, her voice is sweet as honey.

"You will." I chuckle. "If not, Zandian masters have ways to keep our humans most compliant." I lean down and brush my lips across the shell of her ear and whisper, "You'll see."

Her nipples bead up beneath her gown. "What do you mean?"

"We have unique methods to bond human to master," he murmurs. "Don't worry—most humans come to enjoy these methods as much as we do."

I brush my knuckle down the side of her face. "But for now, let's figure out what you need to get you back to full strength. Wait here."

"Not that I have a choice."

Ah. My cock thickens in my leggings. There it is. She's testing me already.

"The correct response"–I catch her chin and hold it–"Is *yes, Master*."

She stops breathing, her gaze wide on my face.

"Say it, Sia," I prompt. "I need your obedience immediately. Now. And every time I ask."

"I..." She hesitates.

I pull her against my body and twist her slightly, tossing the blanket aside. I stroke one hand over her buttock, then give it a mild slap. "You said it before. Say it now."

I scent her arousal as she gasps out a choked sound. "Ai!"

I slap her again, a little harder, this time letting my hand rest after the spank, fingers splayed out across her delectable ass.

"Sia?"

"Yes, Master!" she gasps, then moans slightly and presses her legs together like she needs more friction there. I can't *vecking* wait until I give it to her. But not yet. I need to build trust between us first.

"Good." I rub her ass over the fabric of her gown. "Next time you say it faster, yes?"

"Yes, Master."

"Good girl." I take her chin again. "Because I will spank you for disobedience. Every time. It's really the best way you'll learn."

Her cheeks deepen in color, and she drops her gaze.

Veck. I need to take this little human back to my domicile immediately. I'm rather desperate to start her training.

"I'll return shortly," I say in a rough voice then leave to find out what I need to do to take my beautiful prize home.

* * *

Sia

Sweet Mother Earth!

What's wrong with me that I like that? Why do I want him to do it again, right now? There's a vague memory of being backhanded by Ocretions across the face–that was painful, terrifying. This, however, is like warm honey in my veins.

He leaves me with my racing brain and my quivering body, but the knowing look he shoots in my direction tells me that he knows exactly what his two spanks did to me.

The cell door slides shut behind him, and I know it's locked. But I don't plan to escape. Where would I go? And why?

I stand and touch my ass with both hands. It doesn't hurt, yet there's a slight tingle from the spanks. The need between my thighs has grown, and I feel a wetness at the top of my cleft. That's new—my body has never done that.

When he returns, my face flushes again.

"I've received permission to take you to my domicile," he announces. "You will stay there with me."

"Yes, Master," I murmur. "How long?"

"As long as is necessary." He gives me a measured look. "To regain your memories and acclimate to life here on Zandia. I'll determine when you're ready to integrate into society here."

"Can I speak to my—the other humans before we go? My friend, Flora? Please?"

I need to talk to Flora as soon as possible. Does she remember more than I do? What is the thing we're supposed to keep quiet? Who *are* we?

"Later." He gazes at me. "She's resting."

'Please." It comes out almost a sob. Do you beg a master for this? Because I will, if I thought it would help.

He regards me, and his face softens. "I'll show you."

Instead of taking my elbow this time, he picks me up like I weigh nothing and carries me down the hall then taps a door. It slides open.

Flora is lying on a sleeping platform, eyes shut,

breathing evenly. Her face is battered and bandaged. Her hair still shorn by our masters as punishment. Her skin bears Ocretion tattoos of her crimes–mostly escape attempts and disobedience.

There's a caretaker–a human I don't recognize, one who must live here, adjusting some items on a tray. She nods to Daven and gives me a look of sympathy.

"She'll be out for another few planet rotations," she whispers.

I give a small cry. How will I remember more about myself if I can't talk to my friends?

"Shush." My master talks into my ear. "She's going to be fine, but she's medicated and sleeping. You'll see her again, I promise."

I nod into his shoulder. "All right. Thank you, Master."

I keep my head tucked against his chest all through the journey to his domicile, registering the hovercar, the light from the suns and the beautiful buildings gliding by.

Zandia is truly a magical planet.

This almost seems too good to be true.

It's that suspicion–the notion that my being here is somehow related to my work in that lab and that something terrible is going to happen–that keeps me from relaxing into my master's strong arms.

Daven

The human cuddles against me, almost like she's trying to climb into my chest. She's terrified and still shaky. It sends my protective instincts into overdrive.

Yet she's already lied to me at least once. I saw her look

away when we were talking, and I could tell she was hiding something.

Axe was right. I can't trust her.

But what is she hiding? And why? I'll find out. It's my mission to find out.

I don't mind applying a little gentle punishment to bring her to heel. Human females love it. It turns them on sexually and bonds them to their mate and master. I smile, remembering how her pupils widened and her whole body pulsed with desire when I merely tapped her pretty ass twice. Oh, she's going to be fun to train. And discipline. And own, if only for a short time.

My cock strains against my breeches, and I will myself to calm down. Slow and steady with this one, I think.

She murmurs in her sleep and shifts, and the gown slides off her shoulder, revealing perfect skin and the swell of a perfect breast. *Slow and steady.*

"But not too slow," I whisper. *Veck*, it's all I can do to keep myself from ravaging her right here, right now.

Chapter Four

S*ia*

   I spend a comfortable night with my new master in which he makes no demands of me. He shows me how to use the incredible and fancy washtube, gives me wonderfully soft and comfortable clothing, and has food brought to his domicile for me.

   The next planet rotation, I'm taken to a memory session with Dr. Daneth. Although he's done nothing but help my wounds, he scares me. He's too smart. I feel like he knows I'm lying about something.

   His assistant, Bayla, smiles. "Sia, lean back in the hover-chair and try to relax. We'll just ask you some questions and see if you can remember anything. Yes?"

   I nod. I like Bayla. Human like myself, she's apparently mated to the doctor and holds a position of prominence on the planet with much freedom and acclaim. Furthermore, she seems blissfully happy. I think about Daven and how different it is with us. He's made it clear that we're only together to help me regain memory and because he's my appointed master—nothing more. Once he gets what he wants from me, I'll be released to another master.

"Sia. So far you've told us that you're a tech worker and a slave on Ocretia." The doctor's voice is low and even.

I glance around the med bay, which is clean and sterile, yet not unwelcoming. Low cabinets line the walls, and there's a large window through which afternoon light streams. My cushioned seat is comfortable and plush although my body is still tense with worry.

"Yes. That's right." My heart pounds.

"I'm going to ask you questions, and you try to answer as quickly as you can."

I nod.

"Bayla will fasten this band on your wrist. It won't hurt. It's just going to record your vitals while we talk."

I nod again. A lie detector. My heart sinks. I take a breath and figure I'll do my best.

He asks a series of queries: What do I eat daily? Where do I sleep? These are easy, and I start to relax. These I can answer truthfully.

Then it gets harder in the sense that I'm back in that gray area of what to tell and what not to tell.

"What kind of work do you do?"

I start with my previous tasks. "I was assigned to a lab where I assisted chemists with experiments. Basically I organized beakers and cleaned them and took notes on a holo device regarding ratios." I tap my fingers together, inserting the nails of one hand under the nailbeds of the other. "Yeah."

He and Bayla look at each other. The device on my wrist flashes.

"And? What then?"

I bite my lip. "More of the same. Then, I ah, was placed

in a new position." I feel a bead of sweat start to tickle at the back of my neck, right at the hairline.

"Alpha 2. Daven told us your memories from earlier."

I nod for probably too long. "Yes, but I can't–I don't remember what I did there."

I look at him and Bayla, trying to appear innocent. I widen my eyes in case that helps. "It's, ah, not really coming back yet. Just flashes." If I mix in bits of truth, will that seem more legitimate?

"Such as?" His voice doesn't change.

"Um, I think I was tied down. I do remember pain." I squeeze my eyes shut because these memories are true and they are hideous. "I think they may have wanted to enhance my, you know, muscles and stuff." I gesture at my body. "See if they could make me stronger."

"They have done that before," the doctor says to Bayla.

She nods, face sympathetic. "I know this is hard, Sia, and you're doing so well. Just a few more questions this planet rotation."

As she starts to talk, the strange buzzing happens in my head, the thing that's happened a few times already. I touch my temple and wince.

"Sia, about Project Alpha. How did they plan to enhance you? I feel like you may know more than you think you do. Try to concentrate."

The buzzing turns into clicks and roars in my ears. Then it stops.

"I really can't say." I shrug, hoping I look concerned but empty of information. "I hope to remember more soon." I add, "I really do want to help," and this part I mean completely.

There's a tap at the door, and the doctor turns. "Excuse me. I need to address him." He touches Bayla's shoulder, at once reassuring and dominant, and I yearn for that kind of connection with Daven.

"Doctor, we've received intel that the Karran are going to be doing close runs through the area, ostensibly on route guide and map creation missions. We're concerned that they're really spying for the Ocretions with the intention to get air to surface high res pictures of our planet and assess our capabilities. We need to discuss any masking or cloaking techniques with you and the experts and whether we can dissuade them from the forays."

"Not here, S-"

The buzz is back, and this time it's accompanied by a series of zaps. They're painless, but each time it happens, my vision resets, and dizziness flickers through my body.

I shudder and shake my head. Then I remember–there's a chip in my head. A chip that can be used to fry me from the inside out. I can't seem to remember what its purpose is, but something makes me believe the chip activated to record these words. Mother Earth, if there was only a way to make it stop.

When the door opens again, It's Daven. He nods to me, then he and the doctor confer for a few minutes. The doctor takes my wrist device and checks the readings, then shakes his head while he and Daven continue to speak in voices too low for me to overhear.

* * *

Daven

Sia appears pale and anxious after her session with Dr. Daneth.

Part of me wants to snatch her up, tell the doctor to

leave her the veck alone and carry her back to my domicile where I can protect her from every being.

But, then again, she might be stressed because she's hiding something. Dr. Daneth seems to think she knows more than she's saying and is afraid to talk, but he said her inability to give us clear information could also relate to her head trauma and memory loss.

I'm not sure what to think.

As we're walking out, Axe emerges from another lab room, his large hand clamped around the nape of Flora, the human with the punishment tattoos and shorn head.

She holds her head high, and there's a stubborn angle to her chin, as if she intends to resist Axe, if not bodily then with her mind. Her emotions.

"Flora!" Sia cries when she sees her friend. She throws her arms around the pale-skinned female, and Flora murmurs something in her ear that I can't make out.

"She can't speak to you now," Axe growls, pulling Flora away and sending Sia a dark look that makes my right hand curl into a fist.

But that's foolish. Axe isn't threatening my female.

At least, he'd better-*vecking*-not be.

"Where are you taking her?" Sia's voice is shrill with fear.

"She's all right, little human," I assure her. "You all are safe here on Zandia. Axe won't hurt her."

Axe straightens his shoulders, and a muscle in his jaw jumps. "Of course, I won't," he says stiffly. "We just need answers." He sends another glower Sia's way. "From all of you humans."

"We'll get answers." I sound more positive than I feel, but I don't like the unease dripping from Axe. I don't want it spilling over into my relationship with Sia.

Renee Rose & Rebel West

I'm already growing attached to having her in my domicile. To being her master.

"If they wish to remain on Zandia, they will have to divulge everything. We're not harboring agents of Ocretia."

I scoff. Now Axe is being ridiculous. "No human is an agent of Ocretia. They were slaves. They had to scrape and cower just to stay alive. Remember that when you're questioning your female."

For the first time, Flora turns her haughty gaze, which had been pointedly directed away from Axe, up to his face. She searches for something there.

"She's not my female."

Flora's lips tighten, and she looks away.

"Was she not remanded to your care?" I probe.

Axe hesitates. "She was. Temporarily."

"So you're her master, and she's your charge."

"She's my–" Axe breaks off and sends a quick glance at Flora. His horns thicken and tilt in her direction.

As I suspected. His interest goes beyond the information she may have.

"She's your female for now. Remember what she's endured. If her past made her rebellious, it's because she lacked freedom of any kind."

Axe immediately releases Flora's nape as if her slender neck scalded his hand. "I know that," he snaps. He takes her by the elbow instead. "Come, human," he barks.

"Coming, Master," Flora murmurs in what might be construed as a respectful voice but somehow misses the mark.

Sia reaches for her friend, but I catch her hand to lead her away. "Another time, Sia."

She directs those large, dark eyes at me, blinking her thick lashes. "Yes, Master."

Unlike Flora, Sia sounds genuine, and her velvety tones make my dick hard.

I have ideas about how to make my little human talk, and they all involve her naked and at my mercy.

In fact, I can't wait until I can set aside the time for a personal interrogation. One with a bit of punishment mixed in to keep her honest.

We step out into the sunlight as my friend Khrys and his human mate Kailani walk up with their young toddler in arms.

Sia gasps, staring at the halfling child then at his two parents.

I lift my forearm at a right angle, fist high in the traditional Zandian greeting. "Khrys, Kailani, this is Sia. We rescued her and several other human slaves from Simak 14."

Khrys mimics the greeting gesture while Kailani stretches a hand out to grasp Sia's.

Sia only has eyes for the young, though. "Who is this?" Her smile lights up her face, making me almost jealous of the child for evoking such joy from her.

Making me desperate to put young in her belly, to watch her grow our own halfling.

"This is Nicao, our young," Kailani says with a matching smile. "He's just over one solar cycle."

The tiny young lifts his fist in the air as Khrys and I had, and we all laugh in appreciation and return the gesture.

"He's so smart," Sia coos.

"He's here for a checkup with Dr. Daneth. We would stay to talk, but we're already late," Kailani apologizes.

"Of course. Nice to meet you," Sia exclaims, her gaze still on the halfling.

When they go in, she tips her face up to mine. "So it's true–Zandians do mate with humans?"

I nod. "It's true. Our species is in danger of extinction. Dr. Daneth discovered that humans are the best breeders to allow us to repopulate the planet."

Sia's forehead wrinkles. "But Kailani isn't..." She darts a glance in the direction Kailaini and Khrys went. "She's not just a breeder. Is she? They looked... mated. Happy."

My horns thicken and tilt in her direction. She wants to be mated. To bear Zandian young. I'm sure of it, and the idea makes my blood run south to my cock. I want to be the male to put those young inside her.

As if she catches my mood, she presses up against my body, her nipples tenting the thin fabric of her dress.

"Many humans mate their masters," I murmur.

She blinks, and I catch the scent of her arousal.

"Would you like that?"

"Yes, Master." She adds a purr to her voice.

My horns thicken and pulse.

Veck, yes.

I lower my face to hers, my lips hovering close to her lush mouth. "Show me you're a good little human, and we'll see if we make a good match."

"Yes, Master."

I want to taste her. Disrobe her. Find out what makes her scream. But she's still recovering from her injuries. I'll have to wait another planet rotation or two.

Veck, I want to initiate her sexually.

Axe is so wrong about these females.

They're not to be feared. They're meant to be gently but firmly conquered.

Chapter Five

Sia

"How are you feeling?" Daven asks the next planet rotation.

It's a sunny morning and beams stream in through the large domed window of his domicile. His is a raised abode that overlooks a somewhat busy square below, and like everything on the planet, it's quite beautiful.

A crystal–Zandian crystal, Daven told me–is embedded in a skylight in the ceiling, sending cascades of rainbows across the walls. Daven says Zandians use the crystal energy to nourish their bodies–they barely require food at all.

"I like seeing the beings come and go." I gesture at the road, paved in flat stones that twinkle with bits of crystal. Two humans chatter below me–it's a comforting sound. "I like watching."

A group of Zandian warriors stride together towards a far dome. They are as strong and beautiful as Daven although they don't evoke the same yearning for physical touch in me that he does.

"When will I get to see my friends?" I take a grape from

the cluster he's left for me on the gleaming silver surface. Daven eats only every ten planet rotations or so, but he provides me with the most amazing food I've ever tasted. Fresh food–fruits I've only heard of but never seen or tasted before.

"Soon. After they all have settled."

I'm desperate to fill in the blanks in my head about what happened and why we're here. I know my concerns are legitimate because when I hugged Flora last planet rotation, she warned, "Don't say *anything,* Sia."

I'm not even sure what it is I shouldn't say, but I could tell that she remembered something and that we are not to talk about it.

Now I know it has something to do with the chip.

I'm dying for a chance for a real discussion with Flora and to see the three others–Katia, Alyza and Janae. I'm still somewhat in the dark about the big secret we keep in our heads. What is its purpose? For some reason, I believe it's meant to record things.

Which could be a problem. What if we were sent as unwitting spies on Zandia?

But that doesn't make sense. We weren't sent to Zandia, we were left on Simak 14 by a group of Ocretions who thought we were pleasure slaves. There was a mix-up of some kind. We were shipped to the wrong location.

So where were we meant to go and why?

And what will happen now with these chips in our heads? Can we be tracked? Are they recording?

A shiver runs through me as I suddenly understand why Flora sounded so urgent about me not speaking. I remember what they can do to us if we talk–fry our brains from the inside.

The chip is interwoven with our own neurons.

"I'm thankful to be here," I hurry to add, lest I seem ungrateful. "The food is delicious. I'm safe and warm. But. It's been three planet rotations now, right? May I see Flora and the other humans?" I gesture outside and look up at him. "Please, Master."

He sits beside me, and the warmth of his body makes me tingle, as always. The frustration at being kept inside and the fear about my missing memories fades every time I feel his presence. Every single time he approaches me, the need in my body gets stronger. I want something I can't put into words. It's a different kind of frustration entirely.

He touches my face. "Your wounds have healed externally. But your memories are still lacking. Dr. Daneth feels it's better to keep you mostly isolated until you regain more control over your thoughts."

"I disagree, Master." I stand and pace. I don't know what makes me dare argue with my new master, but somehow I sense I'm safe here. "I think going out would help me. My body is full of adrenaline, anxiety, need. I need something. I need release."

"Have you been logging in your memory journal?" He narrows his eyes at me. "Sia?"

I nod. "Yes. Of course, I log all of them." This is a lie. I have logged many, but I've held back anything that deals with my head scar or the Project Alpha details—not that I've even had much success remembering much about either.

"I had another one earlier. Should I tell you?"

He nods, eyes narrowing, as if he's not sure I'm being honest.

I touch the device, but don't press the play button. "I remember I was in a lab, and some of the Ocretion lab managers were talking. They were excited. They said," I pause and close my eyes to get it right, "that there were new proteins they'd isolated that could be given to us in conjunction with various hormones to get our endurance up and make us heal faster from injuries."

I open my eyes and look at Daven. "They were writing on a holo board, and I remember the symbols. I can scribe them."

Daven has gone quiet but his whole body vibrates with eager interest. "Yes, Sia, please." His voice is low. He hands me a tablet with a blank screen. "Do your best to replicate them."

I don't know how I can do this, and maybe it should scare me because I don't know chemistry. I don't remember all that much about my past, but I know that I was good at organizing glassware and doing basic mixtures, but I was not an expert on science–I was more of a "follow the instructions" tech.

It's weird, like watching a video, and again–like when I first met Daven–I'm shaken about how my brain can play back something so completely, as if I'm watching a holo. I'm pretty sure my memory never used to work like that before?

"How can you remember all of this?" Daven's voice has a strange tone as he watches me cipher–not accusatory, but more than idle curiosity. He peruses my work. "I can't even understand this. Most Zandians don't remember things so photographically." He enlarges part of the screen. "This is very complex."

"I...I honestly don't know."

He examines my face like he's not sure what he sees.

"Daven, I really don't understand how, but I just remembered it. It's just there, in my head." I shrug. "For some reason, I can envision the holo screen in that lab, and remember myself looking up from my beaker organization task, and the symbols locking into my brain."

"Is this a project with which you're familiar? Do you experiment with chemicals?" he probes further, brow furrowing.

"I know nothing about this tech. It's like transcribing a foreign language, but I know it's accurate, at least to what I saw that day. I just–it's in my brain."

"This is good. Very good." Daven finally sounds pleased when I finish the complex series of equations, even though he still seems concerned. "It's a strong memory, and we can try to share it with the other humans, see if it triggers more from them. And if it's true, Dr. Daneth might be able to replicate the techniques to help humans here on Zandia." There's excitement in his tone–and pride. "Excellent effort, Sia. Do more like this."

I flush. I love the feeling of making him proud of me.

"I'm glad I can help." I touch my head. "You and the Zandians have helped me–us–so much. I want to help all of the humans here as much as I can." When I say this, there's a weird flash inside my head and a buzzing. I touch my temples. "I..." I shake my head.

'This one is perfect for Project Alpha.' It's an Ocretion speaking. *'Smart, can cipher, learns remarkably quickly. And brainscan shows all the pliability we need.'*

I'm restrained with straps. We're in a lab. They're going to do the surgery now–the one that is going to be the pinnacle of Project Alpha–and turn us into....

Then myself, much later, reaching up to touch healed scars on my head–scars that match the ones on Flora's skull....

What exactly were we turned into? I want more of the memory, but it doesn't complete. But I remember enough. Something terrible happened to me in that lab, something with the chip, and it's what Flora wants me to keep secret. *Needs* me to keep secret, so we can all stay alive.

"What?" Daven leans in. "Tell me."

I shake my head as the memory swirls, and the dizziness fades. "It's disappeared," I lie.

I don't want to be dishonest with Daven. The problem is that when the flashes come–and they *do* come more often than I admit to him–I don't know which ones are safe to share and which ones are not. I still can't shake that fundamental feeling that I need to learn more about myself before I can tell Daven anything. After all, apparently my life–and Flora's–depend on keeping something secret. I'd be foolish not to give myself at least a little time to figure it out on my own first, right?

This particular memory is clearly not one that I feel safe sharing right now.

But Mother Earth, he can tell that I'm lying.

"I don't think you're being honest with me." Daven's voice deepens. "Sia, as your master, I insist that you answer truthfully."

"But I did." I try to look convincing. Too bad the only thing I can think about right now isn't the stupid memories, but the way he slapped my ass twice in that waiting pod. And how it made me feel. He hasn't touched me that way again, and frankly, I'm dying for it. Being near him awakes feelings I've never had before in my life. Maybe if I can goad him into some action, we can stop talking about the cursed memories. I'd rather not get them, anyway.

He's not fooled. "All right." He slaps his hands onto his thighs, nods, then stands. "We can do this the easy way or the hard way. Frankly," Daven gives me a dark smile, "I'd prefer the hard way. Although you might not."

My stomach leaps. "What's the hard way?" I put a hand

to my mouth. I wanted something from him, but...do I want this?

"Let's find out, shall we?" His voice is conversational.

He heads to a cabinet and unlocks it. "It's about time, I suppose, that we acquainted you with some of the Zandian methods, Sia."

"M-methods?"

He retrieves a black bag from the cabinet and comes back to the hoverseat beside me.

"Indeed." He pats the bag.

I inch away from him. I'm not sure about this.

"Sit still." His voice is iron.

I stop sidling immediately. "Daven?"

"You can call me *Master* right now."

He opens the bag and takes out a small leather strap. "Do you know what this is?"

I stare at it. Shake my head.

"Answer me."

"No. Um, No, Master." I swallow.

"It's a little spanking device, Sia. For your pretty human ass."

I flush red hot. A mix of trepidation and need floods my belly. "I..."

"You," he emphasizes, "are about to get a lesson in obedience. Humans get punished when they disobey their masters. Lying to me is not acceptable."

He slaps the strap into his palm, and the sound cracks out across the room, making me jump.

He smirks. "Stand in front of me, Sia."

Wordless, I get to my feet and obey. I feel like I'm walking in a dream. I'm shocked at what he plans to do, but part of me–that special place between my thighs–is electrified at the idea.

"Lift up your gown."

"But I...." I thought he'd just grab me and do it, like in the pod. My face gets even hotter.

He slaps the strap into his hand again, harder. "Delays only add more spanks, Sia. You'll learn that, too. What I'm asking is not hard. Take the fabric with both hands and lift it up past your waist."

* * *

Daven

Sia's face flushes with confusion and–I suspect–desire. I need to start pushing her–just enough. She's been dodging my questions for the past few planet rotations, and I know she's deliberately not telling me what she's remembering. That needs to stop. I think she's ready for the human training to begin. I know humans are receptive to the discipline when delivered in a sexual manner. In fact, they may even come to crave it. I can only hope that will be true for her as well.

"Sia."

She gulps then slowly takes hold of her dress. "But you'll see my, my..."

"That I will." I raise an eyebrow. "Your panties. And more. Up." I nod my head.

She hesitates. I can see she's torn between her desire to obey and her embarrassment.

I stare at her until she finally starts to lift her dress. As the fabric skims her thighs, she licks her lips, and something flares in her pupils.

Ah, there it is. My little human does like this. I'm on the right track.

"Higher."

She obeys. "That's as high as I can hold it." Her voice is defiant but also needy. Oh, yes—she doesn't even know how badly she wants to be owned.

"Good. Stay like that."

I stand and stalk around her, observing her from all angles. *Veck*, what a perfect little ass she has, two gorgeous pale globes barely covered by the gossamer silk of her undergarments. Her thighs tremble, probably from nerves or anticipation. Possibly both.

"Widen your legs." I slide the strap between her thighs and push at the left one.

She squeals and jumps a little bit, but obeys.

"Yes, Master." She moves her leg out a few inches.

"Wider."

"Yes, Master." Her voice wavers as she steps her legs apart.

"Good." I tap the inside of her thigh very lightly, not a slap, just a touch, and she gasps.

My cock is already rock hard.

"Stay like that until I tell you otherwise. Don't move a muscle." I tap her other inner thigh.

She sucks in a breath. "Yes, Master." It's a whisper.

I take the bag just out of eyesight and begin arranging a few items on the surface of the storage unit. I can tell she's dying to look—her whole body vibrates with a nervous curiosity.

"Master, what are you—"

"You'll find out soon enough." I open the soft pouch that holds the anal trainer. Dr. Daneth said that some humans respond especially well when this device is coupled with a spanking, and I intend to find out.

I walk to the hovercouch and sit down with the strap and the trainer. "Walk over here, keeping your dress up."

She obeys, and I almost catch my breath at how sexy she looks. The panties ride high on her thighs and barely cover her cleft.

Her eyes widen when she sees the silver bulbous trainer glinting in the light from the window, and she blinks rapidly.

"Come closer, Sia." My voice is a low growl.

I grab her waist and pull her closer, until she's right in front of me. I can smell her arousal, and I know that if I touched her between the legs, she'd be wet. She probably doesn't even know why.

Veck, I need to be careful here.

"Over my lap."

She makes a little whimper but doesn't resist as I pull her down over my thighs, keeping her dress draped up over her back and shoulders to present her ass to me.

"Have you been spanked before?" I rub her skin with my hand. It's perfect, like the rest of her. Taut, soft, smooth.

"No, Master." Her voice is low.

I keep rubbing, soft, slow, and she responds by pushing her ass up into my hand. "Have you been asked to present your body to your Master like this?"

"No." Her voice is a little breathier now. "Never."

"Get used to it," I advise her. "I'll be asking for this whenever I want."

She moans.

I take my time, rubbing over her panties, then sliding my fingers under them to touch the skin hidden by the small scrap of silk.

"Spread your thighs a little," I order.

She does it without question. I slide my fingers lower, over the part of her panties that covers her little asshole and even push in a little so the fabric sticks in her hole.

She squeaks, but pushes her ass up again.

Veck, she likes this as much as I do--at least so far. I push my finger again, a little further, forcing the fabric in a little more. Then I glide my fingers down the gusset of her panties. They're soaked, just like I thought.

"Have you been touched here?" I lean down and whisper, sliding my finger up and down the little wet strip of fabric. "Or here?" I tap over her clit.

"No." Her voice has a dreamy quality. She shifts her thighs. "Oh, please. More, please."

I rub gently, so softly it's barely a touch.

She responds instantly with a moan and pushes her hips down into my hand.

"No." I move my fingers. "You don't move, Sia. Keep those hips completely still."

"Yes, Master," she breathes.

I put my finger back on her rosebud. "You like this?"

"Yes, yes." She's breathing more rapidly. "Oh, Sweet Mother Earth."

She pushes her hips again.

"Did I tell you to move?"

"I'm sorry, I can't, it's just... it feels so good."

She shifts again on my lap, and I can tell that any embarrassment she had about lifting her dress is long gone. But unfortunately for her--and for me--this session isn't going to end in sex.

I pick up the strap with one hand and pull on her panties with the other, so they tuck into her ass crack a little more. Tug again, making them taut, until she whines.

"Well, now that you're warmed up," I tell her, "let's see how you like the spanking strap."

"But--" She's confused. "You're touching me." She tries to twist around.

"Correction. I was touching you. Now I'm going to be whipping you." I use my free hand to gently realign her. "Stay in this position."

I raise the strap. "It's going to hurt," I warn. "Because it's a punishment. And I expect you to stay on my lap and keep your hands down, Sia. Is that clear?"

She tenses. I put a hand on the small of her back. "Relax your pretty ass," I command. I drop the strap and rub her skin softly until she does. Then I pick the strap back up.

"Twenty," I tell her, and before she can process the word, I lift the little leather and bring it down firmly across both ass cheeks.

"Ow!" she yelps, jerking her body. She kicks her legs.

"Shh, that was just a starter. It's only going to get harder," I chide her. I raise the strap again. Whap. I make this one harder, quite a bit harder, and it leaves a bright red stripe across her buttocks.

"Daven, ouch!" She twists again.

"That's *Master*, and those two didn't count because you moved. We start again. Stay still, hands down, no kicking," I order.

"I'm sorry, I just–ow!" she wails it out again as I bring the strap down again, this time concentrating on her right cheek.

She kicks again.

"And another one that doesn't count. Let's try again."

I bring the strap down a few times, alternating cheeks, moderately hard.

She yelps and reaches back. "Ow!"

"No hands, Sia. I'm not going to restrain you because you need to learn to control yourself."

"But it hurts!" She sounds surprised.

"I told you it would." I smile to myself.

She rubs her thighs together, and I can see that she's even wetter than before.

"Behave and the spanking ends sooner. Keep fighting me, and it goes on longer. Your choice."

I bring the strap down once, twice, three times. A few more times, alternating hard and light strokes. Probably ten or fifteen spanks.

She squeals and twerks and reaches back again.

I tsk. "Oh, Sia. None of these have even counted, and you still have twenty hard ones to go. If you don't start listening, your bottom is going to be extra sore tomorrow."

She sucks in a breath.

Her bottom is already pink with some red stripes–her skin reddens very quickly, apparently. I know I'm not striking hard enough to damage her, and I want to get that sweet spot of just enough punishment.

"Tell me you're sorry," I demand. "And that you'll be obedient while I whip you."

"I'm sorry, Master," she manages, her voice catching. "I'll be obedient...while you...whip me."

"With the spanking strap," I add.

"With the spanking strap," she repeats. "Master."

"Good. Now we'll count twenty hard ones. Stay still across my lap."

I raise the strap and bring it down hard. It cracks out, and she sucks in her breath but manages not to move.

"Good. That's one."

I spank her again, a little harder. "That's two."

I pause, making her wait. She wiggles. "It hurts." But her voice is breathy.

I make her wait for it. Then I bring the strap down on her thighs a few times before going back to her ass.

By the time I hit twenty, she's squirming and barely staying on my lap–but she hasn't reached back again.

I'm dying to keep going. I want to strip off her panties and whip her until she begs me to stop, until she's promising me anything and everything, swearing that she'll suck my cock twice a planet rotation and let me *veck* her ass anytime I want–but now's not the time. I will play with her ass a little, though.

"Good little human." I rub her ass. "You took that part of your punishment very well. I'm proud of you." I use both hands to soothe her skin, rubbing circles, until she melts into my lap and starts opening her thighs again, telling me she wants more.

"Now I want you to reach back and pull down your panties to your mid thighs," I tell her.

"Why?" She's instantly on alert.

I slap her once again with the strap. Hard. "Your job is to obey, not question." I spank her again and again. Two good ones. "Pull down the panties or you'll get ten more."

"I'm sorry!" She scrabbles around, ungraceful, and manages to get them down. She has to pull them out of the crack of her ass and pussy, and I'm so turned on by the sight that I can barely manage to control myself.

I get her back over my lap. "This," I tell her, picking up the silver device, "is called an anal trainer."

"A what?" She sounds scared.

I push the blue button on the end of the silver device and a smooth, clear gel drips out of the tip. I use my fingers to rub it all around the device then press the button again, so a few drops fall onto her asshole.

She squeals.

I push the tip of the device right at the entrance to her ass.

"I'm going to push the trainer into your naughty bottom, Sia," I tell her. "And then you're going to hold it in while I spank you again."

As I speak, I start to slowly push the device.

She clenches up instantly.

"Stop." I smack her cheeks. "Open for me, Sia. you'll open for me every time I ask."

Her voice is muffled as she mumbles into my leg. "Yes, Master."

She sniffs and relaxes her body.

"Good little human." I stroke her hair, then rest my hand on her pretty ass. "I'm going to push this in slowly while you tell me all about how you're going to obey, understand?"

She nods. I can practically see the red spreading on her face. I smile—training this pretty human is a *vecking* rush.

I insert the device just a bit, and she squeals and squirms. I imagine she's feeling the warmth of the oils Dr Daven infused in the gel, and I hold her firmly. "Sia, start talking. Tell me about how good you're going to be for me."

I edge it in further, and she gasps as her tight muscles are forced to expand to take the bulk of the plug.

"Please, Master. I'll be good," she manages. "Ow! Oh, Daven."

I slap her ass. "And?" I slide it in another inch and enjoy the feel of her body shifting as she struggles with this new sensation. I know it's not too painful, but it's surely like nothing she's ever experienced before, warming her up from the inside.

"I'll obey you and be honest. I promise!" Then she squeaks as I seat the plug fully and give it a twist.

"See that you do," I warn, giving her a spank across both round cheeks. "Because this plug can expand and rotate,

Sia. And it can exude more of the warming gel that will make your pretty bottom feel more and more like it's burning from the inside."

She whines, but I scent a sudden sharp increase in her arousal. I chuckle. "You like this, sweet human. And that's good because I plan to do this to you...often."

She gives a helpless sound and squirms, and I slap her ass again, just because I can.

"Now we'll continue our previous conversation," I tell her. "Back up to the part where you lied to me, and we'll go from there."

Chapter Six

S*ia*

"But I didn't lie." I know he doesn't believe me. I don't even believe me—my voice is utterly unconvincing.

The plug in my ass throbs and hurts, but it's also warming me up, so the wicked spark between my thighs is increasing exponentially with every rough and invasive thing he does. It's like my body was built for this.

"Oh, Sia," he almost croons. "I'm sorry you still need to lie. I did warn you."

He taps the plug. "You ready to start changing your story?"

I bite my lip. "What...oooooh." The plug vibrates in my bottom hole and reverberates through my entire belly. "Daven!" My voice is high and needy. I shift my thighs, let them fall open slightly. "I need...I need."

"What you need,"--he slaps my ass hard—"is to tell me that memory. The one you pretended you lost." He snaps his fingers. "Now."

"I..." I gasp. "It's..."

The memory looms up in my mind again, in full color. *"Is she fully restrained?"*

"Of course. Ready for further testing, Commander."

The room is white with bright, round lights far above my head. Too bright. I don't want to be part of this experiment, but we slaves on Ocretia have no choices at all—we do what we're told, gracefully, or we suffer. "Project Alpha is the linchpin of our future regarding...."

"Talk, Sia." Daven taps the plug again, and the lovely vibration ceases. The plug suddenly expands to a point where it's not really fun anymore.

"Ow." I wince.

"Sia." His voice is granite.

The plug isn't cool anymore, either. In fact, it's warm, and—my ass is burning!

"Ow, Daven!" I reach back, trying to pull it out. "It burns!"

There's a smile in his voice. "It won't harm you, little human, but the botanical extract it exudes can be quite... stingy. Or so I hear. I haven't worn one myself."

"Take it out!" I'm a little panicked and angry. But he's holding me down tightly.

"We do things my way, Sia." He spanks me again, once, twice. "And that means you'll wear the plug on this setting until you choose to tell me the truth. You can trust me. You'll learn that it's safe, little human. The timing on that, though, is really all up to you."

"But it hurts!" My voice whines and catches. It's crazy. My memories may be compromised, but I know I would never normally argue with a slavemaster. Something about this Zandian makes me comfortable enough to show my discontent.

"It will stop as soon as you tell me what I want to know.

Imagine how lucky you are. Some masters make their human females wear the plug on this setting for a whole morning. Would you like that?"

"No!" I say quickly although part of my brain, a strange deep part, wonders if it might not be so bad after all.

But I do really want him to make it do the other thing instead at this moment, the vibration. And touch me. Mother Earth, I want his fingers on my body. I trust that he'll make it feel good.

"Fine, I'll tell you!' I blurt. He says I can trust him, and right now, I believe it. "Please. Okay." I hesitate and continue, "I was in a lab, and I was tied down. They were going to do something to me." The fear starts to swirl in my chest. "I don't know what, I swear, that part is still missing. But they mentioned a project." I swallow, bile rising in my throat. *Don't talk about the work.* "Daven, help!"

My whole body stiffens in utter panic. "I'm not supposed to say it, I'm not, I'm not!" I scream the last part.

He reacts instantly. "Sia, shhh, it's okay, it's okay." His quick fingers turn the plug off, extract it in seconds. "It's okay."

Suddenly I'm in his arms, face pressed to his chest, sobbing. "No, it's not. They're going to hurt me if I say it."

"No, sweetling, they won't. You're safe here, you're not going back. I promise." His voice is harsh, but it's not at me. From him, at this moment, all I feel is protection. "You can tell me. It will only make things better here, Sia."

"O-okay." I take a deep breath. "It's like my mouth won't make the words come out though."

He strokes my back, waits. "Just try."

I take another breath and blurt the thing out before my mind can process what I'm doing. "It's called Project Alpha, and I'm a Project Alpha, and I'm an Experimental, and it's

71

top secret, and those two took us by mistake, and they, they realized their mistake, and they thought maybe they should kill us or hide it or something, and they attacked me when we got to that planet, they were mad and thought we'd snuck ourselves onto that ship or something, but why would we do that..."

I'm hyperventilating. "I don't even know anything else, it's all gone."

"Good job." He strokes my shoulder. "That was excellent, Sia. Thank you for telling me."

He tilts my chin up and meets my eyes. His handsome face is stern, but when he smiles it makes my entire body feel melty and warm. "Well done."

I feel strangely proud and duck my head. "All I did was say something."

"Do you remember more? What is Project Alpha?" He's calm, but I sense the urgency behind his words. "Do you have any idea of what the Ocretions are planning with the Karran?"

I shake my head. "I'm sorry. I don't." Right now it's true—my brain is dancing in my skull, leaping, and all of my thoughts scramble together. And the oddest sensation mixes into it all, like something is alive and whirring—inside my head. What in Mother Earth? Then it fades.

But the worst didn't happen! I spoke about Project Alpha—actually mentioned the words—and nothing happened. I feel such relief that I don't even care about the strange sensations in my head. Maybe things are going to be all right despite everything.

He tips my head up again, and our eyes meet for a few seconds. He nods. "All right. But when you do remember more, you tell me, yes?" He quirks a brow. "Or the punishment will be longer. More thorough." He smirks and suddenly the pangs of desire are back, full force, over-whelming and dissolving any residual fear or angst brought out by the awful memory.

I summon my courage. "I feel like I deserve a reward, though. For being so good. Don't you agree...Master?" I shift on his lap. Now that I'm not caught up in the emotion, I can feel that part of his body is rock hard beneath my thighs. A very interesting part. He makes a small groan, and victorious because I was able to summon that sound from him, I do it again. "You like that, Master?"

Is that my voice, all sultry and slow? Teasing? Where in the mother Earth did that come from?

I don't know, but I do it again. "I feel like we have things to resolve."

He growls and grabs me, and his hands go from tender to powerful in a second. "You think you deserve a reward, do you?" He laughs. "Oh, sweet human, the things you're going to do to earn your release. You don't even have a clue."

"So teach me." It comes out in a whisper, hoarse and wild. "Daven."

I look up at him, at those gorgeous eyes, at his face, and see that his horns are rigid and hard. Entranced, I reach up and wrap my fingers around one. His whole body tenses, and I can tell that he liked it, but he grabs my hand.

"Don't. Touch. Without. Permission," he snaps, but his hand is gentle as he holds mine away from his body. "Understand?"

"Yes, Master." I shift, the need between my thighs impossible to ignore. "Why not?"

"My horns are...sensitive." He clears his throat. "When it's time for you to touch, I'll let you know." His voice is all growly and makes my stomach flip.

"But since you have indeed pleased me, we'll see how

you like this." He reaches down and urges my legs apart. "Have you ever been touched here, Sia?"

"No." I grab his hand, half wanting to push it further, harder against my body, half timid–holding him back.

"What did I say about touching?" He grabs my throat, a firm grip.

I gasp. It doesn't hurt, but I immediately let go. "You said not to."

"Correct," he tells me. "Right now, you keep those hands to yourself. Grab again, and you'll be back over my lap for another twenty hard ones with the strap."

I suck in a breath. "Yes, Master."

He positions me so my back is against his chest and spreads my legs, one on each broad thigh. I feel the cool air of the room on my cleft, and I shudder in anticipation.

"You want something, hmmm?" He trails a finger over my breast. "Let's see if we can figure out exactly what that is."

The nipple pebbles in response, and I writhe, shifting my hips upward. He plays and teases until I'm moaning under his ministrations. I no longer have any desire to push his hands away, not even a little bit. I want them all over me, everywhere. *Now.*

He laughs. "I think you like this." He squeezes softly, then harder, until I moan. "And this." He flicks the rigid tip with his fingernail. "You're so sensitive, *veck*. I think I could make you come just by doing...this." He flicks the nipple again and squeezes until there's a bright pop of pain. I hate it–and I love it. He does it again. And again.

I cry out, arching my body, as sparks of pleasure shoot through my body. It's growing, this amazing feeling. "Please," I gasp, not even knowing what I want him to do.

"Please what?" he asks. He teases my nipples, both of

them now, with his strong fingers. "Please pinch my nipples, Master? Make them hurt?"

I repeat it quickly. "Please, Master, pinch my...nipples." I'm embarrassed to say the words, but I need him to keep doing this. "Make them hurt." But it doesn't *hurt* hurt, not really. It's a clean, good pain that only sparks pleasure. It's unfathomably amazing.

"Good human," he murmurs. "And maybe you'd like this, too?" He runs his hands down my sides, over my belly. I breathe in hard, and his lips nuzzle the side of my neck as his fingers trace patterns on my skin, his breath lighting up my body, so it feels like my whole spine is sending delicious sparks up and down.

I don't know if he touches me for minutes or hours, but soon I can't take it. I need his fingers in a new place, one I've not explored before.

He seems to know. "And maybe here?" He brushes the part of my body that craves him.

I almost cry with the beauty of the sensation. "Stars, Daven, there. Please, there. Yes. Oh stars. Don't stop."

"In case you didn't know," he whispers into my neck, "This..." and he swirls his finger around it slowly, "is your clit. And here..." He moves his finger along my body and ducks it into my opening, "is your pussy. Learn the words, little human. You're going to ask for what you want. Nicely."

"Yes, please, touch me there, on the clit," I moan and arch up, seeking his fingers. His breath lights me up, along with those magic fingers.

"In the future, you'll ask with your mouth," he murmurs. "By pleasuring me so thoroughly that I have no choice but to *veck* you. But for now, this will suffice."

He puts two fingers into me now and thrusts, and I push

back, instinctively moving to make him rub the place that burns.

"Next time you'll wait for it." His voice is a little harder. "I'm going to edge you over and over, and I'll punish you for coming too soon. But this time, we'll let you enjoy it freely."

I don't even know what he means, and at this moment, I don't care. All I want is the crest that's coming. I'm on a wave, and it's growing, and it's going to crash. His fingers move inside me. Another finger strokes my clit, and together they make my body wind tighter and tighter, and I'm going to....

I scream, and the whole world explodes in a starburst of colors and brilliant pangs of pleasure, as my orgasm rips through me, making me shudder with pure pleasure.

It goes on and on until I'm delirious, and then I collapse back onto him, my pussy spasming with joy, skin damp with exertion, quivering with joy. I'm spread open, completely wet with my recent arousal, naked for him—and I love it.

"Daven."

I've never felt anything like it. Who knew life could hold such treasure for a lowly slave like me?

There are sudden tears on my cheeks, but I'm not sad: I'm happier than I've been. "Daven," I say again and press into his body as if it's the only thing I can do. If feeling this good and safe requires obeying his commands, I'll gladly do it every second of every planet rotation. "Thank you, Master."

* * *

Daven

Veck, do I want her, more than I've ever wanted any female. The urge to throw her down and shove my cock into her, ride her hard until I fill her with my rainbow cum, almost has me snarling in desire. I'm so hard it's painful, but now's not the time. She needs to trust me. I'm going to work her over hard next time, that's a given, but now she needs to relax. Trust that I'll do this right.

"Are you crying?" The streaks on her face distract me from my iron hard arousal. I touch a tear. "Did I hurt you?"

Ironic, maybe, but there's a difference between the pain I want to cause and the pain I don't. We Zandians push our humans to a place where pleasure and pain mix but not beyond.

"No, it's not that. You did, a little, but not..." She flushes and looks shy. "You made me feel so good." She sounds reverent. "I've never...my body hasn't...I didn't know."

I smile, filled with expansive pride. Yeah that's *vecking* right. This is my female, I own her and her pretty body, and I gave her that first screaming orgasm of her life.

"You're going to do it again," I promise then add a warning: "But only on my command. Is that clear?"

"Um, yes?" She looks up at me with wide eyes.

I hadn't planned on doing that, but it feels right. "That pussy belongs to me," I growl, reaching down to finger her again. "And this, too." I brush her clit. She's sensitive now that she just came, and she squeaks and jerks her hips. I push back and stroke her clit again, forcing her to take it. "You don't touch it unless I specifically allow it." Yes, this is how it's going to go. I'm going to own her responses.

"But.."

"No buts. Hands back, Sia. If I find out that you've touched yourself without permission, you will be punished. Hard. What I did this planet rotation will feel like a whisper on your ass. And I will find out. Because you're not going to lie to me ever again, isn't that right?"

"Yes, Master." Her voice is high and needy.

I flick her clit, and she cries out, squirms, but she's trapped against me and can't get away. "And I touch you when and where I want, without reservation."

"Yes, Master!" she squeals as I finger her, roughly, then softly. Teasing.

"For example." I run the pad of my index finger over her, again and again, until she's breathing hard. She's even wetter than before, and I can tell she's starting to feel the need.

"Like this." I continue touching, over and over, until she trembles and grabs my forearm.

"Daven, harder, please, harder." She tries to grind against the pad of my palm. "Like this, please," she pants.

I flip her over instantly and smack her ass, hard. "What did I tell you?"

She's startled and stiffens up, so I smack her again. "Relax for your spanking, Sia."

I give her a few hard ones, even harder than before.

She wails and kicks her legs. Her ass is a pretty pink, the stripes from the strap standing out as dull red lines. It won't leave welts or lasting marks—I didn't go that hard. I don't plan on doing that to her, at least not now, but she'll feel it tomorrow for sure. "Daven! Master!"

She's feeling the mix of pleasure and pain that I love to bring to my females. It makes them so compliant and seems to enhance their orgasms significantly. She'll hate it and like it and come to crave it, every time.

I want her so badly that my vision is blurry, but I force myself to make this all about her—this time.

"Let's try this," I growl, depositing her on the sleeping platform. "Spread, Sia."

I pull her thighs apart, and she's only too happy to

help, digging her heels into the covers and arching her hips up, as if she knows what I'm going to do. Still, when I kneel down and put my mouth to her, she cries out and trembles, and I have to grab her thighs so she doesn't get away. It's only a second before she's back to wanting it, pushing her pussy at my face, crying out little sounds that aren't even words.

"This is mine," I growl, licking her slit, tonguing her clit. "All mine. I'll be the one who gives you pleasure, Sia. Just me."

"Yes, Master!" She's barely coherent. Her body keens for the pleasure.

"Don't come," I order. "Hold it."

Then I deliberately swirl my tongue around her clit, in an effort to make it hard for her to resist.

"Daven," she whimpers. "I can't."

"You can. And you will." I reach up and pinch a nipple. "And it will be my pleasure to teach you."

I lick her again, for long seconds, until she's begging.

"Daven, I swear, I'm trying, but it's coming, I can't!" She's desperate.

I'm a little sadistic, I know, but it pleases me to torture her this way.

"So you want another spanking?" I pinch her nipple harder. "If you come too soon, I'll punish you until you cry, sweet human. And that's after you come. It won't be nearly as fun then, you know."

"I know, but I can't!" she wails, her whole body tense.

"Hmm, that's a dilemma then, isn't it?" I make my voice soft. "Let's see how you solve it."

I proceed to use my skills to drive her nearly mad, bringing her to the brink, then pulling back just before she crests. She might think she's holding off–she's trying, but she doesn't know that I'm helping her just enough to let her succeed.

Finally I relent. I lick her to a crescendo of sensation, then demand, "Come for me, Sia. *Now*. Come on my tongue, little human."

And she does. With a scream, she grabs her pleasure and rides my face hard, spreading her delicious essence over my mouth as her whole body convulses in her orgasm.

When she comes down, she babbles something incoherent into my neck. I hold her, and to my surprise, it's only minutes before she falls asleep.

Maybe it's not such a strange thing. I just gave her the first orgasms of her life, and I have to say that they were *vecking* amazing.

I watch her for a moment. Her curls riot around her shoulders, and her ass is pink. She looks achingly beautiful. I run my fingers over her softly, so I don't wake her, forcing myself to stop before I have the urge to wake her and do it all over again. I pull a spidersilk cover over her body.

But my own flesh has powerful needs, and I can't wait any longer. While I watch her slumber, I grab my aching cock and stroke hard, groaning with pleasure as I think about how good it will feel when I finally come inside her tight body. Remembering how wet she got, how good she smells and tastes. When I come, it's hard and powerful and so good that I want to roar and fall onto her, grab her tightly, and never let her go. My little human.

I push that thought away as I clean up and put on fresh clothing. She's not really mine. This is temporary. King Zander didn't give her to me as a mate, he placed her with me for business reasons. It's my duty to bond with her and get her to trust me, give me the information we so badly need. I don't know what will happen once she remembers everything and we give the updates to Dr. Daneth and King Zander. Besides, I know she's lying to me. I can't trust her, even though my body is magnetized by her, and, I have to remind myself, she may be a danger to Zandia. I would never want to even consider taking a mate who's tainted like that. No matter how much I felt like I knew her when we first met, like she was meant for me, that was just my hormones. Or something. After all, I've made big mistakes before, trusting beings I shouldn't have. I won't go there again. Not ever. As much as I can't trust her right now, I can't trust myself either. Let's hope I don't forget it.

Even so, I'm unaccountably satisfied, especially for one who had to self-satisfy, and I find myself whistling under my breath while I tidy up the domicile and work on my tablet, writing down every word she told me about her memories, so I can immediately send it to the king. And even while I work, I can't help glancing at her from time to time, making sure she's still comfortable, just wanting to see her face so relaxed as she dreams.

Chapter Seven

S^{ia}

  I awaken suddenly from unsettling dreams, but they fade fast when I look up and see Daven across the domicile, intently focused on a device in his hands. His broad shoulders and chiseled muscles make me flutter inside, and I want him to do everything again.

"Hi." I feel shy.

"Sia." He gets up immediately and comes to me. "How are you?" He peruses me with a keen gaze. "All good?" He raises a brow.

"Yes, Master. I believe so." I stretch, watching as his eyes snap to my body. He's the master, but clearly I have some power here too. I do it again, just because it's fun to watch him watching me.

He pulls me into his body and drops a kiss on my head, and I want more. He hasn't kissed me yet, not on the lips. I know beings do this, at least ones who enjoy the activities that Daven and I partook of earlier. It's not a memory, but more of a core knowledge. Where I come from, slaves like me don't get mated and don't get pleasure. But we talk about it with each other; some of us have seen things on other planets or in other ownerships. We slaves amass more group knowledge than our Ocretion masters know or would like us to have.

"You should eat." It's not a suggestion. "Keep up your energy. Good for brain healing."

He gestures to a low table spread with offerings for me: grapes, other ripe berries, and some things I don't recognize.

Famished, I tear into the food. "You don't want any?"

He shakes his head. "I could eat it for the flavor, but right now I don't want any."

"You're missing out." I hold up a grape then put it onto my tongue and let the flavor burst as I crush it with my teeth. Teasing him is a new game, and I like it.

His eyes glitter, and I see a muscle clench in his jaw. "No." He gives me a lazy smile. "Not for the things I really enjoy. I plan to get plenty."

I flush because his meaning is clear.

"But for now, I must go." He gestures toward the broad windows, and he could mean anything: war, missions, meetings. "I'll be back by the end of the planet rotation."

He doesn't tell me details. Despite the moments of passion, there's still so much we don't divulge to each other. I still don't know if I can ever tell him the secrets I hold.

"You," he locks his gaze on me, "are to follow my orders. If you get more of the critical memories, you are to record them for me."

"Yes, Master." I bob my head. "I will." *At least the ones I feel safe sharing.*

He waits a beat then sits down close to me. "Sia. Do you like the way humans are treated here so far? Is this better than what you've ever had?"

"You know it is." My voice is raw. "Far better."

84

"Your previous owners, the Ocretions, are known for their cruelty to humans. We're not supposed to give shelter to any, let alone as many as we have. And mating with them, as we do– producing young–they would rather wipe us out, we think, than let us continue with that. It's in direct defiance to their orders. They would consider this the ultimate disrespect and would want to teach us a lesson, so everyone in the universe sees and knows that the Ocretions won't tolerate such behavior."

"I know." This makes my stomach ill. I've been here such a short time, yet I already see it's a utopia. I want to stay here and contribute to this society. To Daven. Desperately.

"So anything you know about their military strength, experimental plans, anything–even if you don't think it's relative or important–could help us anticipate what they're scheming. We can only...."

It's odd, but as he talks, there's a buzzing in my head, like an insect. Except it's on the inside. My thoughts jumble around again like they did on the craft, and suddenly it's like I see his words as ciphered onto a tablet, the sounds coalescing into shapes that I can lock into my memory and download to the implant, *where my master will read it and find out what the adversaries are doing.*

"Ah!" A zap of energy or pain makes me blind, and I grab my temples. "Ow."

"Sia? What is it?" Daven kneels down, face even with mine. "What is it? Your head injury?"

"I don't know." I blink against the intense piercing, spots dancing in front of me. "I can't...I don't know. Hurts so bad." I whimper, but the sound is far away, like a million miles, drifting to me as if a feather in the wind. I slump over.

Then, as quickly as it started, it's over. My head is clear, and the pain is gone. I tilt my head. Something about sounds, shapes? But that's gone, and all I see is Daven's concerned gaze and handsome face. "I'm okay. I think it's just after-effects of the injuries." Something vaguely bothers me, as if there's more to it, but like before, the thought flutters away into vapor.

He looks at my eyes, pauses, nods. "All right. If it happens again, contact me." He points to my wrist, where a comm unit glows. "Push the button, and you'll connect to me directly, Sia."

I nod. "Yes, Master." I smile faintly because the headache is gone, and he's right, life here is glorious, and I plan to partake of it as deeply as I can.

And..." he smiles back, letting his eyes travel up and down my body. "No touching what's mine. Not even one time."

He waits.

"*Oh.* Yes, Master." My face is hot.

"Be good." And he's gone.

* * *

Sia

After Daven leaves, I roam the small domicile, trying not to feel so trapped. I'm lucky beyond belief to be here, and stars, do I know it. Yet, I've already expanded into my new freedom, my greedy soul desiring more, and now I yearn to be outside. To see my slave friends. To do more.

I press a hand to the glass, flattening the fingers out.

Suddenly another image attacks or rather a series or flashes.

"They're up to something. Intel says they have at least

1 0 0 *on their planet. Maybe more. In direct opposition to our orders. The effrontery!"*

I lurch forward, panting, using both hands now to support myself, both palms sweating on the window as even worse memories flood in.

"She's in position. Ready for chip insertion. On my count, doctor."

"Yes, doctor."

"She'll feel pain, but the muscle immobilizer will keep her from moving. She has to be awake while it's done, so we know when it hits the right spot."

"Remember, Sia, those who talk about Alpha Two can be sent to a full week of shock stick punishment. Do you think you'd be as effective at walking and functioning after that? Perhaps a few shocks just to remind you how it feels."

Bracing pain across my entire body.

I scream. Then I slump to the floor, sweating and sobbing.

More memories. *One Ocretion explaining while he waves at me and Flora and the others: These are just experimental for on-planet work. The transmitter will only work within {certain distance}, and the chips are just the rev o. These won't be sent off planet yet.*

And: The last batch of Alphas kept dying when we tried to retrieve memories. Good thing we have such a limitless supply to experiment on." Laughter. Loud, raucous laughter.

That's what I am: An experimental guinea pig. With some kind of chip inside my skull? Is that what makes my head hurt and my thoughts go missing? Why can't I remember more about Alpha 2? I'm just a tool, programmed to be afraid of getting help. Fear programmed into my brain.

I should tell Daven. He can tell the doctor, and maybe they can fix me!

I get up slowly then grab a soft cloth from the wash area to wipe the sweat from my face. I take a few deep breaths to calm myself, letting the panic subside. Daven can help.

Then I realize: *I can't tell Daven.*

Terrible things could happen to me if I tell. And to my human friends. Disclosing this would mean another kind of betrayal, one against myself and my own fate. And one against my friends. The Zandians would surely isolate us, maybe kill us, send us away if they know we have chips. Right? They'd be foolish not to. On Ocretia, any threat was always exterminated immediately, just to be safe. Surely the Znadians will act the same way.

If my memories are accurate, we're far out of chip-reading range. I don't know what else it's doing inside my head, but even if it's recording everything I see and hear, it can't possibly be transmitting to any Ocretions. Zandia is safe even from our spy brains, at least for now. And right now, I want to learn more about myself and Daven before I disclose more. Can I really trust him? Or am I just a tool to him too? A means to an end? Does my life save theirs but only if I kill myself? Do I die no matter what I do? I need time to figure out what my best options are. If only I could talk to Flora. When will Daven allow me contact with Flora? When will he trust me?

When I think of Daven, my chest tightens. Hiding this for even a short time might destroy the tentative bond we're building. But I don't know what the Zandians would do with the information if I gave it to them. They could decide I'm dangerous and deport us all immediately. Then what? Would they send us back to the Ocretions? Trade us to save themselves? I simply cannot take that risk. I want to have a good life, a decent life. And I truly don't think waiting a while longer will hurt Zandia.

The planet rotation passes slowly, and I drift sporadically to the cipher tablet Daven's given me which contains information about Zandia, holos about humans–startlingly fabulous, and I binge on them, watching voraciously until I've seen them all twice. I can't wait to meet the humans who call this planet home, and I hope Daven allows it soon. I also feel a deep need to reconnect with my human friends who were saved along with me, and I plan to petition Daven for that later, when I see him again.

If I'm remembering more about my past and what's lodged in my skull, surely the others are, too. Are they keeping the secret, like I am? Surely Flora is–after all, it's the memory of her imploring me to keep quiet that stuck in my mind. All it would take is one of us to talk, and then we'd be forced to disclose everything, whether we're ready to do it or not. But I can't do anything about it now, and agonizing over the possibilities only makes my heart race, so I watch the holos a third time to distract myself.

After practically memorizing the holos, though, I look out the window and fidget as anxiety grows anew. Strange thoughts prick at the edges of my consciousness, faded images of Ocretions and a lab, and I want none of it. Not right now. I need to learn more about myself, clearly, especially since I've chosen to hide this part of my past from Daven. But at this moment, I think experiencing more visceral memories will maybe destroy me, and I want a break.

I close my eyes and focus energy in the core of my body, trying to force the images out.

"I'm on Zandia now. I'm safe," I say aloud.

At this, there's a sudden zapping sensation in my head. It's painless but powerful, and I gasp in shock. I understand with utter certainty that the chip is recording or transmitting something. Sound? My ideas? Because I said the word Zandia?

"Stop!" I snap, grabbing my temples and squeezing. Nothing changes, and, in fact, the zaps recur, so I squeeze my eyelids and clench all my muscles, including those intimate ones that Daven worked so hard, and suddenly the thoughts and the chip actions pause mid flicker.

When I clench my pussy again, the mental image fades as the tingling sensation grows between my thighs.

Did I do it? Did I stop the chip from doing whatever it does, or did it just stop on its own?

I have no way to tell, so I squeeze my lower core again because that feeling is fantastic, and I'd much rather enjoy it than suffer from the brain nonsense.

Once again, the faint tendrils of an impending orgasm tease the edges of my skin.

Catching my breath, I pulse my pussy experimentally. The tingling increases. Sweet Mother Earth, can I give myself the same sensations that Daven brought forth?

I hurry to the sleeping platform and lie down, my fingers moving quickly to my soft flesh, so I can stroke and rub my clit, which comes to life under my ministrations.

I remember Daven's warning, *Don't touch what's mine*, but I don't stop for a single second. I want that rush and release, so I keep stroking, learning how to adjust the pressure from my fingertips to make the sensation fill and swell. I contort my hips and push up into my hand, crying out in pleasure as I force the orgasm to crest.

When I'm done I lie panting on the soft fabric, enjoying the residual buzz and thrum in my body, and idly wipe a beat of sweat from my forehead. Stars, I could have been doing this every planet rotation! Granted, it was nowhere near as amazing as the one from Daven, but who's going to complain about free pleasure? Not this slave, that's for sure.

Can I do it again?

A few minutes later, while arranging my garments and feeling worn out in the best possible way, I think about whether or not Daven was serious about his edict, and what in fact, he'd do if he found out that I disobeyed him. Now that I've had the pleasure and the sensations have faded, the reality of disobeying a master I care for looms large in my mind. I do care about Daven. I like him. I want to be good for him. It's just–I've never had this freedom or pleasure before.

I consider showering in the automatic washtube, in case he can smell or sense my arousal, but before I can even make a move, there's a sound at the door.

Oh, stars.

Daven is back.

Chapter Eight

Daven

When I enter, Sia whirls, her hand at her mouth. Her face is flushed, and I immediately scent her arousal.

"Sia." I make my voice stern. "Did you touch yourself?" I'm actually amused. I love that she's found her sexuality. I also love the idea of punishing her because it will bond us.

She shakes her head immediately. "No, Master." But the rising color in her cheeks, as well as the unmistakable sweet aroma of her juices on her pretty fingers tells me otherwise.

The little human has disobeyed me, and not even a few hours after I gave her the command. Not only that, but she lies about it.

"Sia. I know what you did. Just admit it." I pierce her with my gaze.

She drops her eyes and fingers the neckline of her silky caftan. "I didn't do, uh, anything, Master. I just watched the holos you left me." She lifts her eyes to mine and meets my gaze. "Seriously." I can practically hear her pulse racing.

"Yes. Just holos!" She bites her lip. "Um, it's good to see you."

Veck. She's the most dishonest little female I've ever encountered. And she's not even good at it. Axe is right to counsel me not to trust her.

I shake my head, my amusement fading to disappointment. Does this human tell the truth about *anything*? Are all humans designed to lie as the default?

Still, underneath the irritation, there's a definite excitement. I'm eager to punish my little charge because we both enjoyed the last session so *vecking* much. Maybe she can't be trusted for a second, but her duplicitousness aside, there's much to enjoy while she's mine. For example, I'm dying to feel her gorgeous pink mouth wrapped around my cock.

"Sia." I make my voice rough. "If you're going to use that pretty mouth to lie, I might as well teach you how to use it to atone for your sins. Right now."

Her eyes widen. "Master?" She apparently doesn't understand my meaning.

Well, she won't be confused for long. It doesn't take too long to explain how to suck a cock. And *veck*, I'm going to make sure she becomes an expert.

"Ah, sweet one, I see that you're not sure what I mean." I move closer.

She backs away. "Daven, I..." Her eyelids flutter in alarm.

"But you will." I reach out and catch her.

She squeaks but melts into my arms when I pull her against my body. I'm sure she can feel how hard I am for her. *Veck,* but this troublesome little female gets me aroused like no other.

Now that she's pressed up against me like this, I forget

all of my mistrust. How can I hold onto it when lust rockets through me?

I reach down with one hand and pinch one nipple right through the thin fabric of her gown. It barely conceals her body, and her flesh hardens under my fingers. As I tease her stiffening peak, she whimpers and winds her arms around my waist, touching my back, then my ass. Nice. I like that she's bold enough to explore my body, and I plan to let her do a lot more although we have something to accomplish first.

"Sia, when you lie to me, there are definite repercussions," I warn her, flicking the nipple, enjoying the way my touch makes her squirm and utter little breathy gasps. She's turned on just by my hands on her breasts. I can't wait to see how high I can bring her with all of my talents.

"But I didn't." Her protest is weak.

In response, I growl and grab the fabric of her dress with both hands and tear it away from her with a satisfying rip that echoes through the chamber.

She cries out and tries to cover herself, maybe shy at the sudden and unexpected nudity, but I grab her arms.

"No. Let me see. You're mine, Sia. Hands down."

I gently push until her hands are at her sides and stare at her lovely form.

I run a finger around her nipple, down the side of her breast, and slowly tease my way to the apex of her thighs.

"Daven," she breathes, closing her eyes.

I touch her clit just once, and I can feel how aroused she is. *Veck*, I think she'd pop off if I just touch her one more time. But I'm not having that, not yet. Sia's going to work for her pleasure this planet rotation. *Hard.*

"On your knees, sweetling," I growl, leaning myself against the edge of the sleeping platform. Then I reconsider: I'm too tall for that angle, and I want to enjoy this more fully.

"Change of plans." I grab her and roll the both of us onto the soft mattress top. I lean back against a pile of cushions and arrange her between my thighs.

"You were told to wait for your pleasure," I murmur, stroking her hair. Her eyes are wide and luminous, and she licks her lips as she looks at my cock. *Veck*, I think she knows what I want, and she even seems to like the idea.

"So now you're going to be forced to wait. Three times, Sia. You're going to give me pleasure thrice before you get to come once. First time will be with your mouth."

"But I don't know how..." she trails off, her gaze nervous as she looks at my size. Truth, I'm large, even for a Zandian.

"You'll learn." I tap her cheek softly. Her mouth is going to be so tight on my cock, I can barely wait to feel it. "Second time will be on your tits, and third time in your ass."

"Wait." Her eyes widen. "You're going to... three times? Before I can?"

She appears dismayed, which amuses me. Is she really so infatuated with orgasming now? I love it.

"But...Daven, I don't think I can wait that long. How long will it be?" She swallows. "I already need to, like, right now."

I laugh. "Not sure, Sia. Maybe you should have thought of that before you let those hands stray this planet rotation. I pick up one of her slim hands, so delicate, and kiss the fingertips. Suck her index finger. "And if I recall, the other planet rotation, you seemed very eager to return the favor after I licked your pussy and sent you into a screaming orgasm. Now's your chance."

She gasps, and I smell her pussy react. She's so responsive. Good. I want her turned on the entire time she serves me—after all, any sexual punishments must be as much sexual as disciplinary.

"We Zandians recharge quickly," I tell her, thinking to reassure her at least a little bit. "But I'm not going to make it easy for you." I raise a brow. "After all, you were patently disobedient."

"What if I..." she tilts her head "If I..." Her nipples are taut, her thighs tense.

"If you come before I allow it?" I shake my head. "Then we start over on my count. Trust me, you're going to want to hold out, sweetling."

Sia

"Go on." Daven's brown-purple eyes have turned violet, and the horns on his head stand stiff and thick, much like his cock.

I reach for his malehood, but he gives a small shake of his head. "No hands. Just your mouth."

"Yes, Master."

I lean forward, tentatively, moistening my lips before I part them.

The head of Daven's cock glistens with an iridescent, rainbow essence, and I flick my tongue out to sample it. I gasp at the taste. Salty and sweet. It somehow affects my body, making me almost light-headed.

His stiff malehood twitches, lurching up in the direction of his head, forcing me to chase it with my mouth. I catch the head between my lips, and it surges forward, dipping fully into my mouth.

I swirl my tongue around the rim, tracing the contours.

His cock is thick–almost too wide to fit comfortably in my mouth, but I open my jaw to take him in, sliding it as far as I can.

"*More,*" he commands, when I draw back.

I lift my gaze to his. His tone was sharp, but he caresses the side of my head with his hand, so I know he's not angry.

I try to take him deeper, bottoming out at the back of my throat. My gag reflex makes my stomach lurch, and I pull back. I go right back down, though, trying again to take him deep into my throat, wanting to please him. To earn his approval and my own release from his skillful hands.

"That's it, sweetling. Let me feel your tongue," he coaxes.

Warmed by his praise, I use my tongue on the underside of his cock as I take him as far back as I can.

"Now lick around the head."

I obey, taking my time licking all around the head of his cock, sucking gently, flicking my tongue over the weeping slit.

"Suck my balls."

I eye the heavy sac beneath his engorged cock. It's glorious. The purple skin is thicker there and ridged. I duck my head to place my mouth over one portion of his balls and suction my lips there to draw one of his balls into my mouth.

He groans.

I continue gently, sucking the ball in and releasing it, then licking all around. I treat the other ball to the same, then lick a long line from the base of his balls to the tip of his cock.

"Good girl."

His praise falls around my head and shoulders like warm sparkles, making me warm and glowy. I lick all over his malehood as if I'm painting it with love. I lick lightly and quick. And long and firm. I blow and lick from balls to cock and back again, making sure every inch of him feels adored.

I've never had a master I *wanted* to please before. I always obeyed out of fear. This is different. I crave Daven's satisfaction with me. I want him to know I'm trying my best even though I don't know what I'm doing. I desire his pleasure.

So I make a study of it—listening to his reactions to each move I make, trying my best to please him.

The next time I take his shaft down into my throat, his hand catches behind my head, and he guides me up and down, controlling my movements. I follow, willingly, exalting in his caught breath, the way his movements grow rough and jerky. His fingers tighten in my hair, tugging it, and he pulls me off as streams of his essence spurt from his cock, spraying rainbows across my breasts.

I touch it, fascinated by the beautiful essence, but Daven snaps, "Don't touch it."

I look up in surprise.

His lips curve. "I need it right there for your next fucking."

Oh. My body buzzes, pussy wet for him.

He climbs off the sleeping platform.

"That's one time, little human." His smile is warm. "You did very well."

"Thank you, Master." I'm absurdly pleased by his approval. I lick his cum from my lips and smile back. He tastes good—fresh, light. I don't mind his essence at all.

His hand is warm on my thigh. It's moments like this when I feel like we're connecting on a deeper level, almost the kind of emotion that could last forever. Of course, we're starting on a false foundation because of my continual lies. I bite my lip as guilt wells up.

"Something wrong?" Ever perceptive, he touches my face.

"No." I force a smile, which doesn't take much, because after all, I am happy here with him. "Just waiting for my turn." I give him a fake scowl and mock hit his arm. "You're mean." Truth, waiting for my release is exciting because I'm anxious and eager to find out what he'll do next.

He laughs, a rich sound, and pulls me closer. "Well, let's...." He breaks off as his comms device beeps with a certain periodic chime. "*Veck*, I have to get that." He sounds disappointed as he gets up from and flicks the device on. "Daven here. Yes, Master Seke."

He stretches idly as he talks into the device, and I'm entranced by his powerful muscles and lean form, all strength and flow.

He puts the device down and grabs his clothing. "Sia, I'm sorry, but I need to go. We'll continue this..." he raises his brows "later. I have to go meet the master at arms."

"May I come?" The words are out before I can think twice. I'm surprised by my own audacity. My risky behavior with Daven is totally new. I am clearly enjoying my newfound freedom. "I'd really like to go somewhere."

He furrows his brow, perhaps debating internally about whether or not it's a good idea, but maybe the recent orgasm softens his mood because he looks at me and says, "You may come."

"Okay! Great! But..." I look down at my chest and the rainbow swirl of his essence. "I...Daven?"

He quirks a brow. "Leave it. The gown will cover it."

"But won't Zandians be able to tell that we...." My face grows warm.

"Perhaps they will." He crosses his arms. "And I don't mind if they do know how I own you, my pretty human."

At my expression, he smiles. "I want my cum on your nice breasts, Sia, just waiting for later. Reminding you that I'm your master. No other being will actually see it, but I'll know it's there. It's going to tickle you a little as it dries, and you'll remember what I did. And what's coming next."

"Yes, Daven," I whisper, arousal growing and nearly obliterating my desire to see the outside world. But it's clear that our bedroom activities are at a halt, so I stand on weak knees and grab my gown to put it on. "Thank you!"

I can tell from the bulge in his breeches that he'd rather stay here, too, but he quickly regains control of himself and takes my hand. "We're going for a short walk to the Command Center. Stay by my side and don't talk to anyone unless I authorize it."

"Yes, Master." There's irritation in my voice, and it surprises me. How quickly I vacillate between utter gratitude at my circumstances and the need for more autonomy!

He slaps my ass once, not lightly. "Learn to behave and tell me the truth, and you'll earn more freedom. Remember that every action has a cost or a reward."

I don't answer, but his words sink into my psyche. I absolutely believe him. It's just that finding the right actions is like walking a minefield.

The day is bright, and there's a breeze, and it's exhilarating to walk outside like a normal citizen. I feel like beings are staring, though, and I shrink into Daven's side. "Are they looking?" A Zandian turns to gaze with a penetrating expression then glances away when Daven makes a little growling sound.

He nods. "Well, they're curious. Everyone knows you're new here."

"What else do they know about me? Us?"

"Not much." His voice is even. "They know you've been assigned to me temporarily and that you'll be reassigned later. So some of the males are probably going to be curious about you. Like that one."

"Oh." All of my good feeling vanishes. I don't want to be reassigned later. In fact, the idea sends a javelin through my chest. I want to be mated to Daven, like the humans I saw in the holos he left me to watch. I want to have young with him. "I see."

"But that won't be for a while," he adds. "So don't trouble yourself about it, Sia." His voice is rough, and he doesn't look at me although his hand tightens on mine. "For now you're mine, is that clear? He won't touch you. No being will."

"Yes, Master." I remind myself that no matter how much I enjoy his company, he has absolutely no plans to keep me once I drain my brain for him. And I need to be ready for him to relinquish me. "It is." I may have glimpses of freedom, but I'm still a slave. I'm not in control of my future, no matter how much rainbow essence I experience with Daven. Maybe it's different for Zandians–not so personal. I don't know if I could feel this way about another Zandian.

We pass some domed buildings along an intricately formed square, and Daven leads me up to the central one in a cluster of three. The dome here is shiny, golden, and reflects sunlight into my eyes. "Fancy." I point upward at the decor. "Looks like jewelry."

He chuckles. "I suppose. Zandians have a great deal of wealth from our crystals, and we like to have our domiciles reflect our appreciation of geometry and harmony."

He holds up his wrist holo to a pad on the wall outside the entrance; a light flicks green, and a door glides open.

"Daven. Welcome. I see you've brought Sia." An older, commanding warrior awaits us. "Come in." He gestures to a cluster of low hoverseats. "I'm glad she's here as well because we actually have a few questions we were going to ask through Dr. Daneth and the memory sessions."

I immediately stiffen. "Questions?"

He holds up a hand. "I am speaking with your master. Wait here, please."

It's not really a request, though, and I sit there alone watching them talk across the room, their big boots shifting on the highly polished floor. While I gaze at them, the skin on my chest starts to tingle. I raise a hand then put it down, face burning as I recall Daven's words: *It's going to tickle as it dries.* The tickle intensifies, and then I start to feel a need between my thighs. Sweet Mother Earth, how am I so aroused just thinking about Daven?

Their voices are low, and I can't make out the words, but as they approach me, I catch fragments: "...Karran scouting for..." and "...it all started ramping up the minute you brought back those slaves from that planet." My head whirs, and I stiffen up, but luckily the sensation fades.

After a moment, Daven returns. "Sia, this is Master Seke. He's going to ask you something."

"Yes." I raise my eyes. "I'll do my best to help."

"First, welcome again to this dome, and we appreciate your help."

I duck my head. "With what?"

"Trying your best to record your memories. We gave the formulas you recalled to Dr. Daneth, and he's quite amazed. He said that the science makes sense, and he's going to synthesize some of the compounds to try out. It's unprecedented that you could recall the formula so precisely."

"I just...it stuck in my brain." But I'm pleased beyond belief that they find my information useful. Although I'm nervous, too–they all seem very preoccupied with the fact that I could remember something so precise. Eventually they'll want to know how and why–as I do. And as I've already figured out, there's something wrong with my brain, and that it has to do with some chip. What will happen when the Zandians discover this, too?

"Well, let's move on to some of the other matters. Sia, there were three other slaves with you, other humans. You all have scars on your head, and in that location, scars typically result from brain surgery. Can you tell me about it?"

My eyes widen. "Um. They performed surgeries on us. To enhance us." Mother Earth, they're already asking!

"How?" His gaze is sharp.

"I don't know. They didn't tell us the details."

"You were part of something you told Daven was called..." He looks at his holo device although I'm sure he doesn't need a refresher. He seems quite intelligent."Project Alpha."

I nod, nerves flaring. He can tell I'm lying; I'm sure of it. "Yes, that's what they called us."

He turns to Daven. "The imaging scans that Dr. Daneth did found no evidence of implants. But the doctor indicated that there might be novel techniques for brain surgery using materials that align more closely with human tissue, rendering the chips nearly invisible to our current tech."

"Sia. Did they ever outright tell you that they were going to implant anything?" Daven looks at me.

I summon all my courage and lie. "I don't have any memories of that. No."

The two warriors exchange a look that could mean anything.

"Are you sure?" Master Seke raises a brow. "You call tell us, Sia. Just like you shared the lab and formula information."

"I trust you. But no," my voice is fast and high, "they never said anything about an implant."

"Okay." They both look at me. Their faces are somber, and Daven is obviously disappointed. My heart aches, and I almost tell him the truth. But I hold back. Not yet.

Seke turns to Daven. "Oh, and Drayk said to remind you that the techs picked up a lot of interstellar chatter, and the one thing that stood out was this: Planet Larew."

As he talks, my brain buzzes again, that weird feeling. And this time it doesn't stop.

Seke continues, "It's associated with Project Alpha. Beyond that we don't know much. See if you can get the techs to refine their searches using best parameters."

Mother Earth, I can't let my head record these kinds of conversations! I need to stop my chip. Even if I'm far out of range, I don't like the idea of something being stored inside me without my control or permission. Because someday, a planet rotation I don't want to think about, what if some being comes to retrieve me and my recorded information?

I clench my core down hard and make myself think about pleasure. Just pleasure. Daven's body and mine together. If I could make the brain chip stop before, in Daven's domicile, I can surely make it happen again.

My whole body resists, and there's a sudden flash of pain, and then my head eases up, and the buzzing stops. I made it stop! I'm ridiculously proud but also suddenly exhausted, and I flinch at nothing and slouch down, eyelids fluttering.

"Sia?" Daven hovers over me in a flash. "You're sweating. What's wrong?"

"Nothing." When he leans in closer, unconvinced, I add, "I, um, had another memory surface." I pull up something to share. "It's about Project Alpha. They said they did want to control us eventually. I don't know how, though. But the surgeries were about making us more compliant."

I figure I can give them bits and pieces of the important info, and hopefully I'll fill it all in soon. Very soon.

"Okay, good." Daven touches my face. "Good job, Sia. I know how hard it is for you to talk about it."

"It's just that they always threatened us if we talked about it at all, Daven." I'm floaty right now and disclosing more than I probably should. "They could kill us, you know. They did kill one slave just to teach the rest of us how it could happen." I shudder. "So I'm nervous."

"How did they do that?" His voice is lulling, gentle.

"They...fried her. Smoke came out of her feet. Electricity of some kind." That's not untrue, and right now my inhibitions are so low. "She was so sweet. She didn't deserve that." Tears well. "None of us do."

Daven strokes my hair. "Shh, I know. You're safe here. Tell me more about the lab. The surgery."

I can see the other one–Master Seke–listening with a stern expression. But I don't care. I allow some lesser memories to spill. He deserves to know some truth, and at least I can give him something, even if I don't mention the chip and what I think it's supposed to do. "Some of us were meant to become smarter, better at lab analysis. Faster. Others were meant to be more powerful, better muscles and tendons. Reflexes. They were just starting on us. New tech, they said, for me especially. It would be a new generation of humans to serve them better than ever, especially if they deployed us."

"Deployed you?" Seke's voice is sharp. "How and where?"

My vision clouds with a pinkish fog, as if I'm looking at things through a dream. The chip buzzes again, and I clench my entire body and focus to make it stop, if I can. Is it possible that the chip can notify the Ocretion masters that I'm overriding it?

"To other places, I guess." My voice is dreamy because I'm so distracted, as the head stuff stops. Once again, I did it! "They said off planet eventually. But not yet and not us. It would have to be the next batch because we, the trial ones, were sort of inferior, not strong enough yet. Not right for the op. We kept dying when they tried retrieving..." oops. Is that something I shouldn't have disclosed? Too late now! My head aches abruptly.

My eyelids flutter. "I'm so tired. Daven?" I turn to him. "I can't do this anymore. My head hurts."

"Retrieving what, Sia?" Daven prompts.

But I can't answer. I just wave my hand.

"It's all right." His voice is low. "I'm taking you home." Daven stands. "We'll head back. And Master Seke, I'll get to work on the things you mentioned. And I'll follow up on..." he gestures to me. "This. What she said."

"See that you do." Seke's voice is firm. "One of the others said something similar. Flora. I'll flash it to your wrist band, the holos of the conversations."

They take leave of each other with a ceremonial bow, and then we're back on the path, where more handsome warriors stare at me. One of them smiles and starts to approach.

"*Veck*," curses Daven. "They're like vultures." He pulls me closer to his side and wraps an arm around me. "Stay close." He leads me away from his fellow warrior, who shrugs and walks away.

And while I know that I did a bad thing by lying just now, I still feel warm and safe in his grip. Like I never want to leave. And the neediness in my body is growing. Veck, as Daven says.

Chapter Nine

Daven

    I suspect Sia lied again. Of course, she mixed in some truth for good measure, but she held back when she spoke of the implant. I have no idea if she actually has an implant or believes she does or what she knows about it. I do know matching scars on the heads of multiple humans don't happen by random accident, so there was clearly a brain surgery done by their previous owners. If the Ocretions are planning to control her–and that part rang true–what better way would there really be than a chip, even though Dr. Daneth couldn't find evidence of any? Why won't she just tell us everything? Why does she persist in further convincing me, more and more, that she's the kind of human that no Zandian can ever trust to take as a mate? Or perhaps even keep on planet?

    Of course, the doctor's tech experts say that there's no evidence of any transmissions coming to or from the humans, so if they do have chips implanted, it's a mystery what they're meant to do, or what they might have done back on their home planet. Why can't she just tell me what she knows? Why can't she trust me?

Then again, does she have sufficient incentive to tell the truth, no matter what it is? Could I do more to entice her? We're not going to resort to torture–that's against our code of ethics on Zandia, and it wouldn't sit well with me anyway.

Maybe I just need to up the level of sexual testing and punishment. She seems to respond to that more than anything else. After all, the only time she really dug deep with honesty was after a sexual episode.

"Sia," I tell her, "we're going into round two. And you're going to tell me some things about your experiences with your previous master."

"Round two?" Her pupils flare, and she swallows. She's aroused just thinking about it.

"That's right." I glance at her as I take off my boots and stow them by the door. "Surely you remember what we talked about."

She flushes. "Um." She tugs at the hemline of her gown.

I take off my shirt. Her gaze rivets to my chest.

"If you like what you see," I toss the shirt to the side, "You should start talking, Sia. I told you I was going to come three times before you do. Where was the second time?" I step towards her with dark intent.

"I'm not sure." She backs away from me.

She's *vecking* sure. She's just embarrassed.

"Sia." I make my voice stern. "Do I need to spank you so soon?"

"No!" She swallows. "The second time...you said..." She lowers her voice and looks at the floor. "My breasts."

"Your tits," I correct. I'm close enough to touch her, so I do: I reach out and pinch one firm nipple through her gown.

"Oh." She breathes in, sort of swaying, closing her eyes. "Daven."

I laugh. "Sweet little thing. Say it."

"My tits." She can barely whisper it.

It's arousing beyond belief to see her so shy, knowing I'll be the one to teach her to overcome those inhibitions.

"And what was number three?"

I pull her to my body and caress her softly, teasing her body, so she writhes against me.

"I...my ass."

I growl. "I may be in the mind to skip ahead, so let's be sure you're ready for me. Let's remove this to start." I tug the gown off her shoulders, exposing those luscious breasts, and keep going until she's standing in nothing but a pair of gossamer panties. "Beautiful."

I pick her up and place her on the sleeping platform. "Knees up, little human. Feet flat on the cover. Yes, like that."

She obeys, looking at me for approval.

"Now show me how you touched yourself before. When you were alone."

"Daven, I can't!" She tries to sit up.

"No, back down." I gently but firmly press her shoulders back until she's lying down, once again. "I'm the master, Sia, and that's an order. Of course, we can utilize the strap for incentive."

I reach for the supple spanking strap that I used earlier. "Shall we?"

"No, I..."

Before she can finish the sentence, I twist her around and pull her over my lap. "Let's start with ten because you hesitated. Next time it will be fifteen." I raise my hand and bring the strap down firmly across both ass cheeks.

She squeals and squirms.

"You know better," I chide, spanking again. "Your job is to stay still and accept your punishment. And say, *thank you, Master.*"

I spank her again.

"Thank you, Master!" she manages as I spank again and again.

By the time I've given her ten, her ass is a nice bright pink; the thin panties did nothing to protect her soft skin.

She moans softly, and I toss the strap next to her and rub her buttocks to soothe the sting.

"Just a little reminder," I whisper, putting one hand on her neck. "Of what happens to naughty little humans."

"I'm sorry, Master," she breathes, bucking her hips up at my hand. "Please forgive me."

Veck, but I already have! My cock is rigid, throbbing to take her beautiful little body.

"Then show me how sorry you are," I suggest. "Flip back over, spread those legs, and touch yourself like I asked."

She hesitates for a split second, but then she does as she's told. Her fingers move tentatively as she pushes aside the fabric of her panties and slides her hand underneath. At first, she doesn't move–she just leaves her small hand there on top of her pussy.

Finally she starts to rub softly. Her thighs are stiff, though–she's nervous.

"It's okay, Sia." I run my hands down her shoulders then move closer, so I can play with her nipples. "Do what feels good. Show me."

I can't *vecking* stand waiting–all I want to do is stick my cock into her tight little pussy, but it's incredible to tease her like this and prolong the suspense for both of us.

Finally she reaches with her index finger and rubs her clit. A small moan escapes her lips, and she tenses up again.

"Keep going," I murmur, flicking a nipple.

"Daven," she whispers. I contemplate commanding her to look at me, but that might be too much for her right now.

For a few minutes, the only sound in the room is her breathing and mine, both of our breaths becoming more labored, as she rubs her labia and clit. At first she's gentle, soft. But soon enough she's starting to thrust her hips up into her hand, and making little breathy sounds like she wants to come.

"That's enough." My voice rings out, startling Sia, and she gasps, her fingers still between her legs.

"Now it's my turn to play. Lose the panties." I flick the waistband of the damp fabric.

She complies, wiggling her body to get them down, then hands them to me.

"Maybe I should gag you with these," I suggest, smiling as she makes a sound of alarm. "But not this time. I want to hear every *vecking* sound you make, Sia. And I expect you're going to be very vocal when I *veck* your pretty little ass."

"But I thought..."

"I said I was going to jump ahead."

"So you don't want...my tits?" She sounds confused, nervous and aroused all at once.

"Well, Sia, maybe I'll press your pretty tits together and squeeze them around my cock, *veck* them for a while first." I straddle her body, moving into position. "You hold them. Yes, little human, like that, just like that."

I help her get the angle just right, then I drive my cock between them. "Missing one thing."

I reach down and swipe my fingers along her pussy, to moisten all of my fingertips. She's so wet!

I rub her own arousal on her breasts, repeating the action until there's plenty of lubrication. "Much better." I thrust in. "*Veck*, Sia, you feel so good." I grunt and push again, enjoying the feel of her delicate skin and firm body. She whines and bucks her hips along with mine, as if it feels good for her, too. As if her pussy feels too empty. I scent her arousal grow stronger.

I think about letting her come, too, but decide that she's going to wait. She was bad, after all, and this is hardly the worse punishment a human could have.

"I was going to take your ass already, but this feels so good, I'll finish here," I growl. "Tell me you're mine, Sia. *Say it*."

"Daven, I'm yours." Her soft breathy voice goes straight to my cock.

"Again." I thrust harder. "*Veck*, Sia, I'm going to cum."

"Daven, I'm yours." She writhes beneath me. "Please..."

I know what she wants, but right now, this moment is for me. I cry out and let the feeling explode, my orgasm lighting up my body from my feet to my horns. I release more rainbow-hued cum onto her body.

"Spread your legs," I order and manage to grab my still-hard cock and press it against her clit. "Just a little taste of what you'll get later," I tell her, letting my final burst of cum decorate her pretty pussy.

"Daven!" She reaches for me.

I take her hands, hold them together, and kiss her mouth once, hard, before rolling over. "Later for you, little human." I breathe hard, just enjoying the sensations, while she curls up against me and puts her head on my shoulder.

* * *

Sia

I'm on fire, and I need his touch. Desperately.

But he's lying beside me, breathing, hand idly stroking my hip, and seems to have no inclination to touch me where I so badly want it.

"Please?" I whisper into his neck, licking his skin. He's a little salty, but I love his essence.

"Oh, you want something?" His voice is warm. "Let's see."

He reaches down, and–*thank the stars*–finally rubs his fingers along my pussy. His cum further lubricates me and makes my skin heat and tingle in an enticing way.

I whine and widen my thighs, trying to entice him to keep rubbing. I let my knees fall apart wide, with no shyness or embarrassment. I just want him to keep touching me.

"We're going to play a game." He stills his fingers.

"A game?" I push up into his hand, vainly trying for more friction. I smell my own arousal and his, and it only makes me needier.

"That's right. Every time you tell me something true from your memories, you get...this." He pushes a finger inside me and swirls it around.

I cry out in bliss because he's almost at the magical spot. "Daven!"

"So start talking, Sia." He rubs me once again, then pulls his hand away and places it flat on my belly. "Tell me about the head wounds."

"I don't..." I'm breathing harder already. "I can't."

"Of course you can. Do you trust me?"

I nod, eyes squeezed shut. "Yes, but it's...complicated."

"Try." He pinches a nipple then swirls a finger over my clit.

"Okay!" I shift, an agony of need inside my body. "I think...I think they somehow altered our brains to make us more compliant. Better slaves."

"Good." He starts rubbing again. "And?"

"And...I don't know."

He slaps the side of my thigh. "Try again."

"I...they said we'd be very useful. They didn't tell us exactly how."

"And?"

"Before the surgery, I was a lab worker. They told me that I was going to do different work from now on. But we were left on that planet before it really started. I don't know what they were planning. I swear it."

"Hmmm." He touches me once again. "More, if you want more." I love the deep rumble of his voice.

I nearly levitate. "I honestly don't know the details of the tech, Daven. I'm not that scientifically trained. And they didn't tell us the specifics."

I'm still not telling him all about the recording details, but at least I'm saying something, right? Then another memory comes to me.

A diet high in Vitamin C and D, along with larger quantities of L-Lysine and MSM, is the right mix to feed them while they're improving brain function. As well as.... The Ocretion proceeds to list out a long batch of things I don't recognize. See that they're all put on this protocol ASAP.

"I remember something!" I gesture to Daven, even though I don't want to think about these memories when he's doing such delicious things to my body.

"Record it, then I continue." He hands me the device.

I barely manage to stutter out what I've recalled into the

recorder, then I turn to him and beg. "Daven, please!"

He seems satisfied because he keeps touching me, and stars, soon I feel the orgasm starting to grow.

I moan as he strokes and teases, and I cry out. "Daven, I need it, please. I know you said three times, but please. I'll do anything, I swear it. Anything you want if you just let me come right now."

He presses his body to mine, and his weight and heat drive me insane.

He bites my neck. "Anything, Sia? That's a serious promise."

"Yes, yes, anything!" I'm desperate.

"Well go on." He pulls back, his eyes glittering. "Let's see what kind of sweet delights you plan to perform."

"Well..." I reach down to touch my pussy because I can't stand it.

He takes my hand and holds it against his chest. "No, you talk first. If I like what I hear, I might relent and let you come before I *veck* your pretty ass."

"You liked it when I sucked...your cock." I'm not even embarrassed to say the words. "I'll do it again, Daven."

He growls a little and pulls me closer.

"Every day!" I'm inspired. "Every sun rise, first thing, I swear I'll take your cock in my mouth and suck it so good, Daven. And if I don't, you can...you can whip me with that little strap until I'm crying and begging you. I'll be so good for you, I swear it. Just please, please."

I wiggle against him, trying to push my clit into his thigh. We're both lying on our sides, bodies pressed together, and I'm craving him. Frantic for him.

He bites my neck hard enough to leave a mark and puts a hand on my throat. "Every sun up, is that right? Without argument or reminder?" He holds gently but firmly.

"Yes, yes, just like the other time!" I reach down to grab his cock, and he lets me. He's so hard it's almost scary, but I love the way he feels in my hand. I can smell his musky aroma, and I love it. I love everything about this.

"You make a very logical argument," he murmurs, licking my ear, and moving his hand to my belly. "All I have to do is a few movements like this," and his hand is back at my pussy, flicking, making me squeal, "and I get my cock sucked every new planet rotation."

"You'll like it so much," I start to say, when he rolls me onto my back.

"You have a deal," he whispers into my ear and kneels over me. "And I do fully expect to find that little mouth around my cock every single sunrise without fail, or I'll spank you hard enough, so you'll be sore all day."

"Yes, yes," I nearly sob, the idea of him whipping me turning me on so much that I could almost come just from his gravelly, growly voice.

"And because I'm so pleased with your imagination, I'm going to *veck* your pussy. We'll save the ass *vecking* for later, when you've been bad."

Why does that make me even more aroused? The idea of being punished by his cock is somehow just as much of a turn on as the idea of pleasure. Maybe because with Daven, it's all one big mix of pain and ecstasy in just the right amounts.

"You're tight," he murmurs, "but so wet. Over time, your body will learn to accomodate me."

I grab his strong thighs and then his buttocks as he lowers his body atop mine although he's using his arms to keep some weight separate. "Daven, I love the way you feel."

"Same," he growls. "Spread your legs for me, sweetling."

I'm quick to obey, and then I gasp as he maneuvers his body to the side and pulls my legs up, bending them at the knees and pushing my thighs, so I'm completely open and exposed.

"Sometimes, I might tie you up for your *vecking*," he says, "but right now you're going to stay in position for me."

The cool air of the room breezes over my pussy, and I shudder with need. "Daven, please."

He laughs. "I love hearing you beg." He puts one finger inside of me and thrusts, and the delicious sensation fuels my need.

"Yes, yes, like that," I urge, pushing my hips up.

He continues, then adds a second finger. And a third.

I moan.

"Too much?" He presses his fingers in more deeply. "My cock is much bigger than my fingers, Sia. we need to get you ready."

"It's too much and not enough. I want you." I grab his wrist with both hands fiercely and pull towards my body. "More."

He chuckles. "Who's the master here, Sia? Do you forget your place?" But he complies, his smile telling me that he likes my sexual demands.

"No, you're the master. I'm your slave, but please...." I contort my body, so I can kiss his neck. It's a little sloppy maybe, but I bite him like he bit me, and he growls, letting me know he likes it.

"Then by all means, let me please you." He expands his fingers a little, pressing against the sides of my body from the inside, and finds a spot that makes me delirious when he presses.

"Daven!" I nearly scream, jerking my entire body, as he

presses and rubs along a patch of skin inside me that is currently on fire with the impending orgasm.

"I don't know if it's enough, but *veck* if I can't wait."

He moves gracefully, and once again, he's on top of me, that huge cock pressing at my entrance.

Although I want him badly, I instinctively clench up. "Sorry," I murmur. "It's just that you're so big."

"Relax your body," he instructs, touching me again.

"I am relaxed." I try and hold my breath, waiting for him to move, but instead he shifts. "Let's try something different this first time, Sia." His voice is almost tender. He sits up and moves back against the pile of fluffy pillows on the hoverbed, his cock jutting nearly straight up, hard and thick.

"You on top," he explains. "Ease yourself down, little human. It will be easier for you like this."

"But I don't know how." I don't care, though and I'm already scrambling toward him, so needy to feel him inside me.

"I suspect you're going to learn fast, beautiful." He lifts me by the waist and positions me the way he wants. "Kneel over me first. Like this, little one. Right here." He deftly arranges my body. "See where I am? When you're ready, you just sink down onto me. And I'll take you to the *vecking* stars."

He growls the last part as he pulls me in and kisses my mouth.

I'm stunned, startled, because he's never done this before. It's somehow even more intimate than the other things we've done, and I love it, press my lips to his. His tongue explores my mouth, and I return the gestures, growing more frantic as he starts stroking my pussy while we kiss. To make it even more arousing, the tip of his cock continually brushes against my clit, sending spires of bliss spiking through my belly and even into my nipples.

"*Veck*, you're dripping for me," he says, his voice full thick with desire. "And you smell so *vecking* good. I want to taste you."

"No!" I protest, terrified that he'll stop touching me, stop this game. "First just let me..." and I position my pussy right on top of his cock. "Let me just..." I relax my thighs just a bit, allowing my body to expand to take him in. "Ride. Your. Cock."

In a burst of inspiration, I reach down and rub my fingers along my pussy, while I sink onto him, then put my fingers to his lips. "Here, you can taste me at the same time."

"Sia, you *vecking* vixen," he snaps, licking my fingers hard and grimacing. "Stars, you're irresistible. I can't take it!" he grabs my hips. "Down on me, little human, Now."

It hurts because his girth stretches me beyond where I've been, but it's also exactly what I want. I'm so wet that I'm able to glide down his cock until he's fully inside me, throbbing and hard.

"Daven," I whisper.

"Are you okay, little human?" He flicks my nipples, then brushes a kiss along my neck.

"Yes, master. Better than okay."

"Good. Then we move. Like this." He shows me, teaches me a rhythm, allowing me to control it by shifting myself up and down along his cock.

"Ow, stars, it's so good," I moan, closing my eyes and tossing my head back as I increase the pace. "Daven, oh sweet Mother Earth, it's so *vecking* good."

It's the first time I've used the Zandian curse out loud, but I like it. It feels good on my tongue. "*Veck* me," I whisper, and in a fit of inspiration, I grab his horns. "Do you like this?" I ask, rubbing.

The sound he makes, a growl of desire, lets me know that he does. Now he grabs my hips and starts to control the motion of our coupling, forcing me up then down hard, impaling me onto his cock. It's too big, but it's perfect because it hits all the right spots inside, especially that one he found with his clever fingers before.

"Daven, I know I'm supposed to wait, but I don't think I can," I cry out as the orgasm starts to build. "Please, may I come?"

"Wait for it," he snaps. "Or else I'll spank you hard, Sia. And I'll make you wait three times for your next orgasm. Maybe four. How would you like to wait for an entire week?"

"No, please!' I'm horrified at that idea and still unable to resist the sensations.

"You'll do as I say," he says, "because I'm your master. You're mine, Sia."

"Yes, Daven, yours, just yours," I repeat.

"Then come," he urges. "Together, right now. Come for me, Sia."

I allow the feeling to explode, and at the same time, I know he orgasms too because I feel a burst of fluid inside me that somehow drives my orgasm into overdrive.

I scream with the pleasure, and it keeps coming, harder and better, until I almost pass out.

Daven shouts out and grabs me hard, probably enough to leave bruises, and I don't care. I want his marks, I want his cum, I want everything.

"I love you," I think to myself. "Daven, I love you."

I know better than to say it, but at this moment, I'm sure of it: this Zandian warrior has my entire heart.

Chapter Ten

S ia
Relaxing together is bliss. I wind my smaller fingers around his powerful ones, then run my hands up his chiseled abs and chest. I find the spot where his hip meets his groin and press. "I like this spot."

He laughs. "That one? I thought there were parts of me that you might prefer over that one."

I put a hand on his cock... still firm! "You mean this?"

He growls. "Exactly."

"That part of you is okay, too." I smile. I'm so sated with pleasure that I might be dripping with joy. "That was amazing."

"It was," he sounds wondrous, almost surprised. "It was."

We're quiet for a minute, but it's not awkward.

"It looks like I've unlocked the secret to getting you to share your memories." His voice is dry and amused at the same time.

I don't want to really talk about this because it makes me sad to think that such incredible sex is just a tool for him to get me to talk, when to me it feels life-altering. So I just nod.

Then I ask something that's been on my mind more and more lately. "Why are you not mated to another Zandian? Or human? I mean, why are you available to take care of me?"

He tenses slightly. "There are no Zandian females. And I just never met the right human to tempt me."

"Okay." I hesitate. "It's just that Axe said. Your friend? I think I remember him saying something on the ship about a previous relationship?" I hold my breath. I probably shouldn't pry, and this is a very sensitive topic. "When you rescued me? You were talking?"

"*Veck*. You remember that?" He takes a breath. "Well, that's not untrue. I, ah." He clears his throat. "There was one...being. But it was a while back. And things didn't end well."

"How?" I sense this is important. That it matters more than he'll admit.

"Sia, this is old history." His voice is irritable. Then he relents. He stares at the ceiling of the domicile as he speaks. "There was a human, Illiana. We had rescued her from a slave auction."

He stops speaking, and I just wait for him to continue. I sense that this is a very important topic to him, maybe more critical than he'd admit.

"We bonded." His voice is flat. "And I promised to make her my mate. This happened very quickly." He takes a breath. "We were still on the alien planet. But it seemed..." he shakes his head. "At the time, it seemed natural. It made sense. We really got each other. Illiana was her name. We spent six planet rotations together, hiding out with the team, preparing to escape the planet. And I was crazy about her."

"Hmmm." I want him to keep talking. Already I hate this Illiana, for the simple fact that she ensnared Daven's heart. "So what happened?"

"What happened." He says it like a statement. "Is that we were hiding in some outbuilding, ready to make a run for a craft, another vessel, since ours had been destroyed. This was dangerous, Sia—I wasn't sure we'd make it. She saw some of her previous captors and called out to them, told them that we were hiding. That she had valuable intel about us, and she'd only been with us to get knowledge."

"Oh, Mother Earth. She didn't." I put a hand to my mouth, outraged. "But why?"

He shrugs, still not looking at me. "Stars, who can know? Perhaps she thought we were outnumbered, and she'd be recaptured anyway, so she decided to throw her lot in with them? Or maybe she really was just tricking us the entire time? It just seemed so...real...what we had together. I cared for her already. Very much." His jaw clenches. "And she seemed to reciprocate."

"That's awful." I touch his arm.

"We Zandians fought off the attackers and got a craft. Escaped—without her. She had made her choice at that point, and we needed to save ourselves."

"I'm so sorry." I stroke his shoulder. "What a horrible being."

"It was my own fault for trusting her so fast and so completely. I should have known better. I do now."

He looks at me, finally, but his eyes are hooded and distant. "I swore to myself that I'd never endanger Zandia or myself again by trusting an unworthy being. My loyalty is to my king and my planet. That will never waver. Ever. I endangered that mission because of my misplaced trust." He shakes his head. "I dishonored myself. It is shameful."

"It wasn't your fault." My voice is low. "You can't hold yourself responsible." My belly fills with unease, and my chest aches. I've already lied to him so many times; he knows I'm unreliable at best. If he has any sentiment for me at all, he'll obviously put it aside in a heartbeat because I'm not honest. And I can't blame him. I would too.

"Of course I can. My duty requires it." He shrugs. Then he looks into my eyes. "So, Sia, I need you to be upfront with me. Tell me the truth about what you've remembered. The things we both know you're not saying. Show me that I'm not hurting my planet by trusting you. By allowing you here in my domicile. On my planet. My home."

The words sit between us and grow in the silence until they reverberate in my skull.

I have to make a choice.

I open my mouth. "I'm telling you everything I can."

Chapter Eleven

S*ia*

    After everything I tell Daven, I share how much I want to see my friends, and he rewards me with a visit.

I'm dying to see Flora and Katia alone for the first time since we've been brought to Zandia. I need to find out what they know and what they've said–or not said–to their masters.

But when I see my friends, those thoughts take second priority over hugging them.

I rush into Flora's arms and grab Katia into the embrace. "Oh thank the stars, you're all right!" We're all laughing and crying.

"You look so good, both of you!" Flora grabs me and examines me, touches the gossamer gown. "So pretty. Your face especially is so light and happy. Oh, Sia."

"Well." I nod. "Daven, my, ah, master–he's taking good care of me, I guess." My face feels hot.

"Good care?" Her blue eyes widen. "Sia! Are you...have you...did you and he do the mate?"

"I think they did!" Katia points. "Look at how pink she's getting."

I laugh and blush further. "Well, it's not called *doing the mate*. And not exactly. But he's..." and I launch into a description of exactly what Daven has done. It's a little weird to discuss it, but it's also fun to have something so phenomenal to share. So different from the things we shared when we were lab animals for the Ocretions.

"Oh, Sia, that's amazing." I detect a touch of yearning in Katia's tone. "My master is very cold. He's so handsome, but he looks away from me all the time. He's barely touched me once, and that was just to help me when I stumbled." She forces a smile. "It's still so much better than our old life, so I don't even care. It's not a problem. It's completely fine. Really, I don't care."

"Oh, Katia. I'm sure he'll eventually...." Although who can be confident about that? "I hope, at least, that he does."

She shrugs and looks away. "It's fine."

"How about you, Flora?" I ask, remembering how gruff her master seemed.

She shrugs. "Axe hates humans, so there hasn't been any mating of any kind. Yet."

"Yet?" I laugh at Flora's smirk. "Do you want there to be?"

She shrugs. "He is quite fine. You know, muscles and smooth skin, and all that. And he wants me. He just hasn't admitted to himself yet that he does."

"Mmm, I can't wait to hear how this develops."

"But we have more important things to discuss than breeding," Flora says.

Right. The thing we should have talked about first. Here I am, frivolously speaking of sex and attraction when there are far more pressing things that can affect us humans.

"Have you two," I take a breath, "talked about, you know?" I tip my head. "The...chip." My heart pounds, and I touch my head.

They both say no, immediately, on top of each other.

Flora shakes her head. "No. You know I never will. We can't. I'm the one who made you swear not to."

Katia agrees. "It's too dangerous. You know what could happen."

My voice is shaky with relief. "Good. Me neither. If the Ocretions ever find us, we could be fried, like Mandy. We need to be so careful."

"Right," Flora says.

"I know. Poor Mandy." Katia frowns.

We all shudder, remembering. Mandy was a test subject too, and they practiced on her, making her crack, just to show us what they could do if someone disobeyed. When they pushed the master button on the auto remote to kill her chip—not just disable it but to destroy it—her whole body went still, then the light went out of her eyes. She fell to the floor, a little smoke coming from the soles of her feet, and they took her away. We never saw her again.

'That,' our master declared, 'Is what we can and will do if we find out that you violated the silence protocol.'

"But I think here on Zandia, it's safe. There's really nowhere else in the galaxies we could be this safe," I say.

"No." Flora appears alarmed. "It's not safe."

"We're so far away, though." I tap my foot, over and over. "I remember hearing them talk about the technology. I know the remote activation can't reach this many clicks away. We must be hundreds of thousands of clicks from them here."

Katia purses her lips. "Are you sure?"

Flora grabs my arm. "We can't be sure. What if they

came in a craft looking, just trying to sync up with our chips wherever we are in the galaxy? And when they locate us, they upload all our info and then kill us?"

"It seems like a low chance," I try to reassure her. "They'd have to actually land on the planet. And the Zandians would never allow that."

Katia shakes her head. "The Ocretions are stubborn and wily. If anyone could locate a pin in an ocean, it might be them. And we're very valuable. Maybe we should tell the Zandians? They could find a way to protect us?"

"No!" Flora's more vehement than I've seen her. "You have to be quiet about it. All of you." She leans forward. "If the Zandians find out we're potential spies who can't even control our own brains, they'll kill us themselves. It's the only logical thing to do. You don't want that for yourself or the rest of us, do you? Now that we've finally found safety?"

I lean forward too. "Of course not! But maybe they would help us, not hurt us."

I think of Daven and my promise to always be honest. Guilt wells up.

"If we tell them, they're smart. They have resources. Maybe their doctor can get the chips out of our heads. Or come up with a plan..." My voice trails off. The problem is that I, too, worry that we'd be killed or banished. Trying to argue the opposite doesn't help.

"You know the chips are intertwined with brain matter, Sia." Flora's voice is flat. "Even the experts on Ocretia agreed that once they're in, it's permanent. They can't even remove them."

Stars, she's right. The memory starts, and I start to murmur along. *"Once the chips are in, they're never coming out. They grow into the brain matter, which is what makes them so perfect. Undetectable. The perfect human recording technology."*

Katia mouths it too. So does Flora. We stare at each other.

"You have that same memory?" Katia's eyes are wide.

I nod. "It's from the lab. It's like–the memories are so vivid. Like holos in my brain."

Flora's eyes narrow. "Do you think it's the chip?"

"I actually do. I think our chips are playing back random things that we recorded back on that planet while they were testing and calibrating the signal."

New memories fluctuate and undulate in my mind, dirty serpents that make me shake. *We own your mind, Sia. Now and forever. You'll be a perfect recording device.*

The chip will record everything we want to learn about. We can wipe your memories after we retrieve them.

"So what should we do? We can't get rid of the chips. And even if the Ocretions can't read what's being recorded, the chips are still doing stuff. I hate it." Flora scowls.

"I know. The only way to be free of the tech is to deactivate them from the control panel back on Planet Larew. Remember they have that master module where they can completely deactivate any chip? They said it was in case of emergency, if their spies were in danger of being found out. They can auto kill and lose everything or just completely deactivate and save their human property to reactivate, as long as we're within range. So if we could get back to that planet and deactivate ourselves? We could halt the whole program. Deactivate it at once!"

"It's impossible." Flora frowns. "How would we get there? Fly ourselves in a starship?" She snorts. "As if we weren't under total guard anyway. iIt's not like we've even been on a craft before."

"Except for our rescue." I think about Daven, bending down, saving me, and my heart melts.

Flora nods. "Right. So right now we have to be quiet. Promise me. For all of our sakes."

"I feel horrible about continuing to lie. Don't you?" I give her a pleading look.

"No," she says sharply. "I don't feel horrible about staying alive. It's our only chance."

Katia agrees. "How can it really harm Zandia, after all? We're out of chip range. For now, we're all safe." She squeezes my hands. "I just hope the Zandians are not recording us talking now."

I give a dry laugh. "Maybe the Zandians are recording us talking about our brains recording us talking. It's quite a concept." I hesitate. "I don't think they would, though. They seem so honorable."

Katia chimes in. "We just need more time, me especially. Once I get my master to trust me and lo–care for me, at least–maybe we'll have more sway. Especially if we keep sharing the useful memories. We can convince them to save our lives, not banish us for being brain-chipped monsters. Please."

I nod slowly. "I don't want to be banished."

"--or killed" Flora interjects.

"Or killed, either. I like it here." I think of Daven, and my chest grows warm. I more than like it here. I absolutely adore it. "We'll do our best to fit in here, make them trust us. Value us. They seem to like the memories I share, the safe ones. About chemicals and technology."

"Me too! I gave them some info about some tech stuff I didn't understand but could transcribe from my chip, and they loved it." Katia smiles.

"Yes!" I squeeze her hand. "Any memories you can get

off your chips—about chemicals or human anatomy or star-ships—share it all. Everything that seems beneficial. Just not that we have chips. And in the meantime, I have an idea about how we can maybe fix ourselves."

Flora frowns. "How is that even possible?"

"We can make ourselves safer. I think I can sometimes make the chip stop doing...whatever it does. Do you get that brain zap thing when it activates?"

She nods, eyes wide and brimming. "Yes."

Katia gasps. "It does! All the time."

"Well, have you ever..." I take a breath and explain the special feeling Daven gave me—the orgasm. "When I tried to mimic it on my own, or at least focused on the pleasure, I disrupted the chip's activity. The whirring stopped."

"Huh," Flora says doubtfully.

"It did. Try it for yourself."

"How, on my own?" Flora sounds startled. "You can just do that?"

"Yes. Put your fingers between your legs and find the places that feel good. Stroke or rub them. It helps if you're thinking about your master—or whatever excites you."

Flora's face flushes, and her brows shoot up to her hair-line. "Um. Okay. If it works. I'll tell the others to try, too." She shifts on her seat, as if already wanting to touch herself.

"I've already tried doing that on my own." Katia blinks. "Next time I'll see if I can use the feelings to stop the chip buzz thing."

"Well, it's something." I sigh. "If we can learn to make the chips stop, that way we'll be less dangerous." My voice trails off. I think of Daven and how much I care for him already. "I just don't want to endanger them," I mutter.

"You *can't* tell your master *anything* about the chip,"

Flora reminds me. "Even if he does things to you. That you like." She narrows her eyes.

I flush. "It's complicated."

"It's really not." She scowls. "Apparently other humans also have done the mating with their masters. You all seem to be so, so happy." She crosses her arms. "Am I disgusting for a human?"

"Flora! Stars, you're beautiful." I grab her hand. "Maybe he'll warm up to you."

"Maybe."

"Just keep the secret, Sia. No matter what."

And it's at that moment that I see Daven arrive with another Zandian.

Daven's face is impassive. "Sia, it's time for us to go." He nods at Flora and Katia. "I trust you had a good visit?"

Katia whispers, "He can't take his eyes off of you. You're lucky."

"Quiet," I whisper, and I think I see Daven's lips quiver although he doesn't outright smile. Zandians must have better hearing than we do.

Flora's master, Axe, is shorter than Daven but more muscular, with an angled jaw and deep eyes. "Come, Flora." He crosses his arms and glowers at her. "If you deem it worth your precious time." I assume there's some history there–next time, I'll ask her more.

"Absolutely, Master." Her voice drips with condescension. "Anything you command."

His expression becomes more stern. "I've about had it with your sassy retorts."

"Oh, really? What are you going to do about it?" Flora shoots me a look and mouths, "Wish me luck."

I roll my eyes. "See you soon."

Flora may be about to get what she thinks she wants.

Chapter Twelve

S*ia*

"So, Sia, we'd like you to meet some beings and share with them some of the memories you've been having, the ones about crafts and tech." Daven leads me toward a small group of beings seated on a cluster of hover-chairs in a small room inside a large tech dome.

This outing, we went the opposite direction of the pala-tial dome where Master Seke seems to work–to a hub of domes near an airfield. On our short walk over, I could see a craft shimmering on a tarmac in the distance behind protec-tive barriers and workers moving around them like bees in a hive. But right now I forget about all of that because amidst a group of Zandian pilots is something incredible that doesn't seem to fit in with the rest.

"Mother Earth, is she a fighter pilot?" My mouth is open as I stare at the human female in front of me. She has a riot of thick red hair tied over one shoulder to reveal a slender neck. She looks delicate but the expression on her face is one of power and confidence, and when she stands, I see how she gauges me, the room, everyone. It's the same way Daven observes the world. This human is clearly something special—a warrior. More special than I am, for sure, with my broken brain and lies.

"I'm Mirelle." She comes up, and to my surprise, hugs me briefly, and I feel how strong she is under her combat suit. "Yes, I'm a pilot. A freedom fighter turned Zandian warrior."

"She's one of our best." A tall Zandian warrior puts an arm around her, possessive. His horns tilt in her direction.

Mirelle smiles at him, and I can tell immediately that they're mated—and seem blissfully happy.

"I am." She nods up at the powerful warrior. "He's my commanding officer—and one of my mates. We go on missions together."

"Wow." I fold my hands together in front of me. "I was, ah, recently rescued. I remembered something about Vitamin C and humans that I told Daven." Stars, I sound like an idiot. I yearn to be as vibrant as she is, so clearly a boon to this planet. How can I become like her?

"I heard!" She seems thrilled by my trivial recollection. "And about the other things, too. You clearly have a really phenomenal memory. Daven said you have some things you recalled about ships that the Ocretions discussed? He said that talking it over with us—with me—maybe would help you recall more?"

"I'd be happy to try," I offer, genuinely praying I can uproot something beneficial from my rattletrap of a skull.

"Let's sit down! Tell me more about yourself," she enthuses, leading me to the hoverseats.

I can tell that she's trying to make me comfortable, but with all the Zandians staring at us, I feel on display. I clutch my arms across my chest and bite my lip.

"Um." Is all I can manage.

Mirelle looks at me then shoots a look to her commander who tilts his head then nods. He suggests, "Daven, how about we leave the two humans alone to converse? Mirelle is more than capable of recording anything critical."

The Zandians confer, then all of them leave the two of us alone. And I feel immediately more relaxed.

Mirelle laughs. "It can feel sort of intimidating at first, I know, so many Zandians around." She has a gorgeous smile. "But you'll get used to it."

"How did you get here?" I'm so curious about her story.

Her face clouds briefly, and as she tells me her history, I ache. Every human female in this galaxy has a world of pain in her past, and Mirelle is no different.

"But I understand that you are remembering lots of interesting things about the Ocretions?" She asks it in an open-ended way, leaving me room to talk.

I nod. "Well, yes. Recently, I've been having some memories about new cloaking protocols?"

She leans in, eyes sparking. "Really? Because that's so critical, Sia. Right now the Ocs don't have the best cloaking around, and we can still find their craft even when they think they're hidden. But if they improve," she shakes her head, face somber, "that could be disaster. We rely on being able to locate them at all times to keep our planet safe."

I clench my gut and close my eyes. If I do it just right, I can get my chip to play back what I want, while not allowing it to record anything new. It does require that I focus in a powerful way, and sometimes, I lose the threads. "Should I draw the things they were showing?"

"Why don't you just tell me what you overheard?"

"Well, it was more me watching. They were pulling up

blueprints on a holo while I was in the room. I think I can recreate it for you."

"Um, sure?" I can tell she doesn't expect much from the disappointment in her voice. "If you think you can." She doesn't think I'll be able to draw anything valuable. After all, how could a random human just be able to draw engineering diagrams from memory? It does sound crazy.

But she hands me a tablet. I take the stylus and close my eyes for a second.

"Okay. The first thing was this." I start at the upper left corner, closing my eyes every so often to clarify the details. Then it's just like copying. "They put these equations down, see, like this?" I cipher faster, as I get used to looking at my brain–as if it's a flat screen–and then transferring it to the tablet. "Sorry some of this is sloppy, these are symbols I don't use or understand. I'm trying to put them down like I saw them."

I keep going, filling up screen after screen. "And then this diagram, here." I work hard to get the lines and angles right, and I'm not sure it's perfect, but at least I'm doing what I can.

When I glance up, Mirelle's face is slack with wonder and intense with concentration. "Sia, how are you doing this?" She sounds almost scared as she points at my work. She pulls the tablet closer. "*Veck*, this is new tech. I think they're–oh stars, I need to get this to Master Seke immediately." She speaks into her wrist device. "Domm, Daven, you need to get back here. This is critical information that Sia remembered!"

She looks back at me. "How can you possibly remember all this if you've never studied it?"

"I don't know. Daven asks me that too. I just do. Maybe

it was one of the enhancements they did to me. Gave me a better memory." I can't tell her about the chip, of course.

But after such concentration, my head aches. I was able to prevent the chip from recording, but it tried several times, and fighting it wearies me.

"I need to rest." I lean back on the hoverchair. "That hurts my brain."

"Here's fluid. And fruit." She brings me some snacks and sits beside me. "Sia, what you just did–I don't know any other humans with memories like that."

"Oh." I eat the berries, grateful for the sweet zap of energy they provide. "I guess to me I'm used to it?" There's a big question in my voice though, and she can tell.

"Sia, did they do something bad to you, your old masters?" She touches my hand. "If there's something you're afraid to tell us, I want to assure you that every being here will look out for you and protect you. We're all one hundred percent dedicated to keeping Zandia and the beings here safe from every threat, no matter how big. Or small."

Her eyes are earnest, but I look away. What if I'm the threat, all the saved humans? What if we're the bad thing, and as soon as they find out we're chipped, they'll send us away?

"I..." I look at her almost in supplication. "There are things I'm scared to say. Do you understand that?"

"Of course, I do. I was a freedom fighter. I've rescued humans from the worst kinds of situations. I'm sure you've been through hell. But Zandia is safe for you–I promise."

Wow. A freedom fighter. Mirelle truly is an exceptional human.

"When I first came here I had a hard time trusting my

mates. It took time." She smiles. "It gets easier. Just try to bond with Daven. You can trust him."

Just hearing the name Daven makes my pulse skitter. Bonding with him is my favorite thing. And I do trust him. I just wish I could be completely certain it was safe to tell him everything. But I can't.

Her attention is pulled back to the tablet, where she scrolls through the things I transcribed. "Stars, I just can't believe this! I can't wait to get this into our systems. This is really phenomenal stuff, Sia. You're like a hero for providing this. And anything else like this you can give us? It will truly help Zandia."

I nod. "If I remember more, I'll save it all."

Then I look right into her eyes. "Mirelle, if the day comes when I need your help to do something good for Zandia, will you assist me? I mean, if it's really urgent?"

She looks at me for a beat, then another. Finally she speaks. "Yes." Her voice is low. "I won't want to do anything that can get you or me into trouble. But I understand about humans, Sia, and the difficult predicaments that we can have. So yes. If you come to me, I will do my best, within my means. That's all I can promise."

"Thank you."

I feel unaccountably better, like I have an ally here. Not that she'd be my ally if she knew that I'm a chip-ridden potential spy. But if anyone seems to care about helping humans help Zandia, it's this female.

The door swishes open, and Daven comes in. My body instantly reacts to his presence, my breath catching in my throat. I stand and when he smiles at me, heat rushes through my body.

He beckons to me. "I hear you've been a great help to Zandia."

"I'm trying," I say, truthfully. When I reach him, he wraps me up in his arms, and I melt against him. "I want to help."

I lift my gaze to his, and he strokes my cheek. "Thank you, Sia. Just tell me everything you remember."

I fight back the sense of impending disaster as I nod, swallowing. "I will, Master."

Daven

I love the way Sia's dark head jerked up when I entered the chamber, those warm brown eyes instantly riveting to my face. She has bonded to me, just as every being promised.

I heard what happens when a Zandian warrior employs sexual dominance with a human female, but now that I'm seeing it with my own eyes, I haven't stopped marveling. It's a wonder to have this female's complete attention whenever we're in the same chamber. The way her body responds to mine. One stern word or look from me, and the scent of her arousal fills the room.

She likes my punishments. Craves my touch.

I crave her, too. Every moment of every planet rotation.

When I'm away, I look forward to coming back. And it's not just for the sexual pleasure. It's the sound of her voice. The brilliance of her smile. The steady way she's attuned to me, so all I need to do is give a subtle shake of my head or nod, and she scurries to please me.

And now she's really starting to give us useful information. She's proving she's trustworthy.

I'm ready to petition King Zander to allow me to

formally mate her. To pierce her skin and embed my crystal as a mating gift and forever mark her as mine.

Her expression now is bright. She's happy. New human rescues are stunned to discover human females with extraordinary skills like Mirelle. And Mirelle isn't our only human fighter pilot. There's Cambry and her brother Tal, as well.

Sia comes to me and throws her arms around my neck in greeting.

I chuckle, banding an arm behind her back to pull her small lush body up against mine. "You enjoyed meeting Mirelle."

"I did," she breathes. "It's so amazing to see what humans can do on Zandia."

Seeing the joy on her face does something to my chest. I find myself cupping her cheeks and lifting her face to mine for a kiss. It's a long, slow kiss, my tongue stroking between her lips, then plunging between them aggressively.

When I pull away, she's breathless. My horns are thick and tilted in her direction, same as my cock. She lifts her gaze to my horns then reaches for one.

I shudder with pleasure when she touches it. "Not without permission, little one," I remind her, but there's no sternness to my tone.

I want her to touch my horns. I want her to kiss them, to lick them, to suck them between those ripe lips.

I slide my forearm under her ass and pick her up to straddle my waist. "Let's go for a ride."

She loops her arms around my neck, and her lips brush one of my horns. I bite back a groan. "A ride?"

"On my ship. I'll let you fly."

Sia's full lips part in surprise. "Truly? Oh! But I don't know how."

I chuckle. "I'll show you. Humans can do anything on Zandia so long as they contribute to society. You seemed excited that a human could fly. Let's see if it's something you wish to pursue yourself."

I carry her out to my smaller fight ship and buckle her into the seat beside me in the cockpit. Her gaze travels over the instruments, and she smiles as I talk her through what each one does.

I take off, but once we're above the Zandian atmosphere, I allow her to take the controls for a while. She sends us into a few swoops and spins that I have to correct, but there's no real danger, and she knows it.

When I land, I turn to her. "Well, what did you think? Do you have a future as a fighter pilot?"

She smiles and shakes her head. "I don't think so, but thank you for letting me try." She reaches for my hand. "It was fun."

I twine my fingers over hers. "I like to see you happy, Sia."

Her eyes brighten with tears.

I frown. "Why are you crying?"

She shakes her head. "No, these are happy tears. Your words mean something to me."

"Mean what?"

She swallows. "You care for me–I mean–do you?"

My chest feels too full. She's right. I care for this little human. She's come to mean everything to me.

"I do." I lean over to cradle her cheek and kiss her again. "I want you to become my mate." I say it before I have time to reconsider. To wonder if I'm being too hasty again. "Would you like that, little one?"

"What does it mean?"

"It means I would pierce you with my crystal, and you

formally become mine. Forever. You'd bear my young, and we'd become a family."

"Yes!" she laugh-cries. "Yes, I want that, Master."

Something in me changes. The anger of Illiana's betrayal melts away. The concern that Sia will do the same or that she's purposely holding something back fades.

She wants to be my mate. To bear my young. If that's true, nothing else matters.

Whatever her past may hold doesn't matter. I believe she will continue to share what she remembers. She wants to help. She wants to belong to me. I trust my feelings about this.

"Come." My voice is gruff with need. I pluck her from the cockpit seat and carry her from the ship and onto my hovercraft.

"Are we doing it now?" The excitement in her voice is what does me in.

I should petition King Zander for permission first, but I don't want to wait even another moment before I claim my little human.

"Yes."

I speed to my domicile and lift Sia out of the craft. "Go inside. Take off your clothes and kneel on the floor to wait for me," I instruct.

Once she's inside, I call Master Seke, my commander on my wrist comm. His holograph springs into the air in front of me.

"Yes?"

"I'm mating her."

His brows shoot up. "You're telling me or asking?"

I don't know what's gotten into me, but I refuse to ask for this. I've already decided, and nothing will stop me now—not even Master Seke. Not even King Zander.

"It's the right thing to do. She's already living as a mate. She wants to bear my young. Whatever secrets she still keeps, I will eventually extract them all."

Master Seke inclines his head. "I will back you on this."

"Thank you, Master." I bow to his holo before he ends the call.

Then I go inside to mate my little human.

Chapter Thirteen

S ia
    I tremble with excitement. The very act of stripping and kneeling for Daven has me feeling submissive and sexy. Owned by him.

I can't believe he's going to mate me tonight!

I've wanted this but didn't dare believe it would happen, especially because Daven always seemed to be holding back. The idea of us becoming a family changes everything. It creates a safety I didn't feel before.

The sense of belonging here on Zandia.

The situation with the transmitters in our heads can be managed. My friends will learn to control theirs the way I have. And if that can't be done, well, now we know a human pilot. If I have to, I will ask Mirelle to fly to Planet Larew, so I can deactivate the chips from the lab.

Guilt stabs at me. Daven is my mate, and I'm still keeping this from him.

Perhaps it's time to come clean. Bring him in on it all.

But not tonight.

I don't want to ruin this special moment.

He enters, the handsome planes of his face rendering his expression inscrutable.

Still, I can tell by the thickening and tilting of his horns that the sight of me kneeling here arouses him.

He walks over and stands above me. "Good girl. Take out my cock."

I rise up on my knees to bring myself eye-level with his waist. He's in the traditional Zandian warrior garb–a white tunic and white pants made of a finely woven material that probably cost more than a hundred human slaves. He uses one hand to pull off his tunic as I lower the pants enough to free his erection.

"That's it," he praises me.

I wrap my fingers around the base, aiming his length in the direction of my mouth. I part my lips.

"Wait for permission," he warns.

I remain suspended, lips open, face inches from his huge, purple member. A drip of rainbow pre-cum leaks from his slit.

"Slowly," he commands.

I extend my tongue and flick it over his slit, tasting his essence.

His cock jerks in my hand, and Daven gives a growl of pleasure.

Emboldened, I run my tongue around the rim of his head, following the smooth contours, and tracing the thick veins.

I cup his heavy balls before I take his length as far into my mouth as I can.

Daven growls and fists my hair, using my head to move me forward and back over his cock.

I love that he controls the movement. Shows me what he likes. Directs the action.

He thrusts deeper, bumping the back of my throat, making my eyes water, but I work hard to relax and keep sucking. He groans as he picks up speed.

My nipples tighten, my pussy soaks knowing he's aroused. Close to finding his release.

"*Veck*, Sia, I smell your arousal. Do you like pleasing your master?"

I pull off long enough to say, "Yes, Master," and then return to my duty.

He tightens his fingers in my hair. His balls draw up, and he climaxes, spilling his seed into my mouth. My throat.

I swallow it down and lick my lips as he caresses my face.

"Did you like pleasing your mate?" His voice is soft.

"Yes, Master," I whisper.

"Sweet girl." He picks me up and gently arranges me on my back on the sleeping platform. He leaves me to go to a drawer, where he pulls out a gun and fits it with something.

"Where do you want to wear my crystal?"

I've seen other humans with piercings. Some in their noses, some ears, some in the sides of their cheeks or eyebrows.

"You choose," I tell him.

He climbs over me, tracing his finger lightly over the contours of my face, then down my throat and between my breasts. "I want it to be somewhere everyone can see. So they'll know you belong to me."

He fingers the crest of one of my ears. "Here." He places the mouth of the gun to the flesh of my ear and pulls the trigger. I jerk at the momentary pain, but Daven's mouth is on mine, kissing away the shock.

"Now you're mine, sweet female," he murmurs. "My mate. My little human. Future mother of my young."

Tears spill from my eyes. "I'm so happy," I sniff.

Daven smiles. "Spread your legs, beautiful. This time I want that pretty pussy."

Chapter Fourteen

Sia

The next day, I go to meet my human friends in the aromatic Cresta tree grotto. As a newly mated human, and having earned Daven's trust, I'm allowed on expeditions like this alone. I can hardly believe my fortune, even though guilt tugs at my gut each time I see him smile. I'm still keeping secrets from him, and that makes me ill.

But at this moment, I'm eager to see Flora and Katia. The last time we met up alone, we all were thrilled to discover that each of us had been able to use my techniques to stop the chip from recording. And even better, the others were also able to recall some interesting information from their own chips and pass that along to their masters. I'm positive that things are going perfectly. Soon enough, we'll be completely safe here, and will be permanent trusted members of Zandian society.

As soon as they see me, they flock forward with cries of admiration.

"What's in your ear?"

"Is that a mating crystal?"

I touch my ear, still loving the feel of the crystal. "It is. Daven mated me." My face warms at the memories.

Flora reaches forward to touch it but pulls back. "Can I?"

I nod, shyly. "It doesn't hurt anymore. It feels nice. Go ahead."

"It's gorgeous! And you're glowing. Just so happy. It shows." She gently touches my crystal. "I'd love one myself, someday." Her voice is longing, but she still smiles.

Katia nods. "Oh, Sia, you're a role model for us all. We can all have this someday." She waves her hand at me. "A relationship, a mate, all of it." But suddenly her smile twists into a grimace. She cries out and grabs her head, then topples over, as if made of rags. As she lies on the ground, she twitches a little and goes still.

"Katia! What happened?" I cry out, bending down to touch her face.

Flora hovers over her in a panic. "Katia!" She grabs Katia's hand.

But our friend doesn't answer—she just clutches her forehead, and her eyes squeeze shut. Small moaning sounds and gasps seem torn from her throat and a fine sheen of sweat coats her neck and cheeks. A tiny pink insect buzzes close to her nose, then darts away.

"Sia, it's the chip." Flora's face is pale despite the warm day. Her wide gaze blazes with both anger and fear. It's an expression I've seen on her before.

On a planet rotation burned into all of our memories for an eternity.

"What happened?"

"You know what it is. Same as Neera." Flora kneels beside Katie, holding her hand. "Remember? She called out that her chip activated, and then she collapsed."

"It's the chip? Are you sure?" I drop down, too, and touch Katia's shoulder. She's still alive–so it's not like Neela. That's good. "I thought we all figured out how to make it stop."

Flora's expression is a grim panic. "I don't know! I guess she never got that good at it. Maybe she was lying when she said she could do it." She looks away from me. "I didn't want to tell you because I worried you'd say something. And we wanted more time. I should have told you."

I nudge Katia again, once, then harder. "Wake up. It's us, you're okay, Katia, please!"

She cries out, "My chip! I think it's activating!" Then she shudders, pulling away from me, trying to curl into a ball. Pollen from the trees mixes into her hair. I brush it aside, then flinch as my fingers touch her skin.

"Mother Earth, she's so hot." I pull my hand away from her face. "Did you feel her?"

Flora doesn't seem to hear me. Her gaze darts around like a cornered animal, but there's nothing unusual in sight. "Is there an Ocretion ship up there?" She looks to the sky, but it's empty except for the bright Zandian star. Not that we could see into orbit, anyway. "Are they coming for us after all this time?" Her voice is so trembly, I can barely understand her. "I was so sure we were safe!"

"I don't know!" I whirl my head in frustration. All we see are the Zandian trees around the recreation area, and the flowers, and in the near distance, the square. I can't even see Daven although I can summon him with my wrist holo. He's always nearby when I interact with my human friends.

Flora looks like she's ready for battle. "We have to do something. We're not letting them kill her."

I shake Katia harder. "Wake up. Katia, please, tell us what's happening."

But she can't. Her whole body goes still, then floppy, and her breathing is labored. Then raspy. Her face begins to turn a bluish-gray.

"We need help." I stand, my heart racing. "I need to–we need to tell someone what's going on."

"No. There has to be another way. Remember what they'll do!" Flora grabs at me, her nails sharp on my arm.

"We're past that!" Anger at her, at myself, at the whole situation well up. "They're already doing it! She's dying," I shout. "And it's our fault because we decided to keep our past a total secret. And if they're up there," I point wildly to the sky, "and get close enough, then yes, they can maybe wipe us all. Or get the info that's on our chips, whatever got recorded before we figured out how to block it."

"Maybe we should just let her recover by herself." Flora's voice is low. "Maybe it's not the chip after all." She pulls my arm. "Maybe she's just feeling sick! Our heads hurt all the time and buzz and do weird things. It doesn't mean the chip is really activating! She's just panicking."

For one microsecond, I contemplate this. Could we say she fell and hit her head? Hope that everything works out for the best? But when I look at Katia's face, I know she needs help immediately.

I've had enough with the lying. I know what I need to do. I push my holo button. "Daven!" I cry, hearing the absolute panic in my voice. "I need you. Help me, please." I stand up, craning my neck to spot him, and relief flows through me when I see him running in my direction.

It's only seconds before he's at my side, eyes darting to Katia but landing on me first, checking me. "Sia, are you all right?" He touches my face once.

The concern I see in his eyes slays me. This is the very

last time he'll look at me that way, with care, before he finds out about my colossal lie.

I grab his hand, hoping to communicate without words that I care for him, I'm sorry for everything that's about to happen. "I'm fine. It's Katia. She collapsed. She needs help."

He drops down and touches her neck, finds her pulse. Then he barks commands into his comm and turns back to me. "I've summoned the doctor and the staff. We'll get her help. Did she eat something new? Has she been ill?"

"No." I bend down. "It's not that. I..."

There's a flurry of activity as several warriors run up with a team of medical staff.

"It's...there's something I need to tell you." I can't even look at his face. The guilt is so overwhelming that I want to vomit. "And you're not going to like it. I'm sorry."

"Secure her head, she's starting to seize."

"Quickly, put on the sedation patch and get out the analysis kit."

"What happened?" Daven, starting to sense something, maybe, takes my arm. And the grip is less personal than I'd like. "Sia. Talk."

"It's her chip!" shouts Flora, hands on her hips, angry tears swimming in her eyes. "Her brain chip has been activated, and they're going to kill us all!"

"What?" The icy tone in Daven's voice is so powerful that I flinch. I manage to look at him. His eyes are wild. "Sia, what is this about a chip?"

I take a deep breath. "Daven, We have implants in our heads that were put there by the Ocretions. I never told you. I wanted to. But I was afraid it would kill me. They've been trying to record information, and it's possible that if the Ocretions are in range, they could activate the chips to upload data and find our exact location." I swallow and add, "And they can remotely kill us, too. We're not safe if they're within range. But it was only supposed to be within 15,000 clicks, I swear!" My voice is plaintive and weak–how strange that something so small can kill an entire relationship. Because in front of me, as Daven starts to realize what I'm saying, I can see his whole demeanor change until he's looking at me like I'm a stranger and like an enemy. "I really think we're out of chip range–they'd have to be literally standing on the planet. But apparently, Katia said something about her chip activating, and then she fell."

"Let's get her to the Med Center," someone barks, and the medical team loads Katia into a hovercar and whisk her away.

Several warriors remain, including Daven and Master Seke.

"All this time, there have been chips in your brains that are recording everything?" Daven's voice is cold.

"I don't know if they get everything. I'm pretty sure they were coded to record when they heard keywords like *Zandia, humans,* and other things."

"And have the chips uploaded anywhere?" His voice is urgent. "Think, Sia. Fast." He squeezes my arm harder.

"Ow!" I cry.

He drops my arm but keeps me pierced with his gaze. "Sia, have they uploaded?"

I shake my head. "I don't think so. No, not if we're out of range. I'm sure."

"How could you know that for sure?" he roars. "You should have told us immediately! We could have made you safe. Made us all safe. Now we're all at risk!"

I shrink back tears making my vision wavy. "I'm sorry. So sorry."

"*Vecking* stars, they could compromise our whole plan-et," snaps Seke. "Put them in the dungeon where we can block any incoming or outgoing transmissions. *Now*."

"Yes, Commander." Daven stares at me, but his expression is blank. It shows nothing. No love. No anger. Nothing.

Oh, stars. My worst fear has come true.

I'm dead to him.

Chapter Fifteen

Daven
     My whole body turns to stone. *It's happening.* It's happened again.

I put my faith in a human female, and she's betrayed us all.

"How long have you known about this?" I demand as I catch Sia's arm to bring her to the dungeons.

She stumbles along beside me. "From the...beginning, almost. Pieces. I remembered pieces and then put it together with Flora. I didn't tell you because I feared something like this. And I'd promised Flora from the beginning. We were threatened with instant death via the chip if we ever talked."

The thought of what happened to their friend Katia happening to Sia cracks the granite in my chest for a moment.

Veck, if anything happens to her...

But it doesn't matter. I can't keep her as my mate. Not after what she's done. Why didn't she trust me?

Sia continues to explain herself. "Daven, I was afraid

your king would not allow us to stay. Or would order us to be destroyed. But I've been trying to figure out how to make it stop!" She turns pleading eyes on me, but I refuse to look. "I was going to tell you just as soon as I figured out more. I learned how to make it stop recording, and I taught them. I hoped we could deactivate them completely."

"Clearly you didn't!" I snap. "Katia is proof of that."

"I don't..." She shivers, like she's cold.

"You may have killed your friend with your silence, and you jeopardized all the rest of them—and us..." I sweep an arm wide. "Zandians with your lies. *Veck*, Sia." I run a hand between my horns. "You betrayed us all!"

"I'm sorry, Daven. I was scared. We were scared of what you'd do if you knew. And I really believed we weren't a risk because we were so far from them. I thought I could come up with a plan."

I stop and turn to stare at her. Does she really believe the words she's saying?

"You—a human female with no resources or freedoms—you were going to execute a plan by yourself, something better than all of the Zandian warriors and intellectuals could create? Had you told us, we'd have our best minds on it!" I start walking again, tugging her along beside me.

Behind us, warriors escort Flora, Alyza and Janae.

Sia's face crumples, and I scent her tears. "I'm sorry." She stumbles, probably because she can't see for the tears.

Veck, if those tears don't take another chink out of the stone casing around my heart.

"Daven, I am so very sorry. I didn't know what to do."

"Anything but that would have been acceptable. Sia, I gave you so many chances to talk to me. To tell me the truth. Wasn't I good to you?" My jaw feels too tight to speak.

"You were," she sobs, making my chest ache. "But I was

so scared. I didn't know what to do. I didn't want to lose you, Daven."

I struggle between the urge to gather her against me and soothe away her pain and the knowledge that she can't ever be trusted. She's not a suitable mate for me. When will I learn?

I must renounce her.

We march to the dungeons in silence. When we reach the stairs, I remand her to the guard there.

"Take them to a holding cell," I command. "They are a danger to Zandia."

"Daven, wait," Sia cries, her fists balling up in my tunic.

I pry her fingers free. "I can't keep you," I tell her, working hard to keep my voice steady. My heart hard. "I can't keep a female who is a risk to Zandia. A female I can't even trust. I don't even know you." I say it again, more softly. "I don't know you."

I turn away and nudge her toward the guard. "Take them now."

Every step I take away from her grows heavier. Harder to drag. By the time I reach the palace steps, I feel heavier than a battleship. Older than the Zandian star.

I punch the nearby hammered metal wall hard enough to leave a dent. It glints in the sun, further enraging me. My hand barely hurts, and that makes me angry, too. I want to hurt.

The warriors nearby turn and stare. It's unusual for a Zandian to experience big emotions. At least, it was until humans came to our planet, changing all of us.

It seems now I've changed, too.

But what have I become except broken?

Twice betrayed?

I punch the wall again.

I treated her well. I honored her, I cared for her. I was good to her. Why would she continue to lie? I stare at the ground where the wind has swirled the dry dust into whorls. I thought we were making progress. I thought she was starting to be honest with me. Why wouldn't she just tell me about the danger she was in?

I answer my own question. Because humans are duplicitous creatures. All of them. And I wasn't smart enough to catch that she was hiding something so critical. I failed. Again.

Memories of the last time I trusted a human flood into my brain. *Veck*, did I learn nothing from my first mistake?

Now Zandia's at risk and...

And I'm without a mate.

Sia is no longer my mate.

Veck. I don't know how I will survive without her.

Chapter Sixteen

Sia

I can't keep a female who is a risk to Zandia.

Daven's words echo in my ear for the remainder of the planet rotation.

He's not keeping me. I'm no longer his mate.

Nothing—no outcome—could be worse than this one.

Not even death by chip.

I was just trying to keep us alive, but what if Daven was right? Katia might die because I didn't speak? Why did I value my promise to Flora more than my commitment to Daven?

I haven't heard yet if Katia still breathes.

The room I'm locked in is smaller than the one I lived in upon first arriving, and it's chilly, probably from the shielding materials. Also because it's subterranean. It's not awful, but neither is it pretty, and although I have a sleeping platform with a cover and there's a small bathroom facility attached, I'm alone. And scared.

Food was delivered through a hole in the door last night and this morning, but I have yet to see any being.

I bang on the wall, hoping to maybe connect with Flora, Alyza, or Janae, but my fist makes no noise at all on the thick concrete, and I give up immediately, collapsing on the cushions and bursting into noisy tears.

How did things get so bad so quickly?

Well, my lies didn't help, that's for sure.

I wrack my brain trying to come up with an idea about how to fix things with Daven, but there's nothing.

First I need to fix things with Zandia. I need to prove we're not a threat. That we can be trusted. That we haven't, nor will we ever, betray Zandia.

The only way to do that—other than to offer our lives up for them to destroy the chips and our brains with them—is for me to get to Larew to deactivate all of our chips.

With all of my might, I focus on the chip and the memories stored there. Stars, there are so many things I recorded while they trained and tested me. Things they'd never in a million sun cycles let a slave like me hear—except they thought of us as dumb and disposable. Probably figured we'd be dead within a short time. Maybe they were just sloppy.

As I strain my brain for anything related to Larew, a whole batch of new memories unlock.

"Stars!" I gasp. "I remember it all!" Passcodes to the lab buildings, the entire layout of the facility, the guard changes. I overheard—and clearly recorded—all of it while they were working on me.

"I can do it!" I cry to myself in excitement. "I can make it all go away! I know how to deactivate all of us from the main panel!"

Then my heart sinks. Even if Daven—or any being here—bothers to listen to my new memories, they will hardly trust me now. It would be dangerous and foolhardy to travel to Larew just to deactivate all of us. Now that Daven hates me, he'll probably petition to have me banished. Surely no being here will actually take on the risk of traveling to an enemy planet for this!

"Daven!" I scream, even though I know he's not near, and nobody can hear me through the thick dungeon walls. "Please, I'm sorry, and I can fix it!"

I hear the beep of a lock activating, and the door swishes open. I leap from the bed hoping–stupidly–it will be Daven. Did I summon him with my fervent pleas, somehow?

It's not Daven.

It takes me a moment to realize that the being standing there is the answer to my prayers.

Better than Daven. No, that's not true. Nothing would be better than Daven, but she may be my answer to restoring Daven's faith in me.

It's Mirelle. The only human pilot I've ever known.

I fly at her, embracing her as if we are old friends. I half expect her to shove me away, but she doesn't. She accepts the embrace for a few moments before she gently extricates herself.

"Mirelle! I need you," I gasp.

"I thought you might," she says. When she catches my surprise expression, she explains, "You mentioned something when we met."

"Yes! Yes, I did. I need your help. My friends and I have been surgically altered. We have chips embedded in our brains. The only way to deactivate them is to get to the control center on Larew. The lab where I worked. I was the lab tech. I assisted the scientists who worked on this tech. I know how to disable the chips."

Mirelle's eyes narrow. "If you knew how to disable the chips, why didn't you do it before?"

"They would have killed us all! I was never left alone or unattended. And I had no confidence in myself. How could I have done such a thing?" I shake my head. "At the time, I wasn't ready to do such a thing."

"So what makes you think you can do it now?" Mirelle crosses her arms and examines me with calculating eyes.

My stomach knots, and cold sweat breaks out between my breasts. "I don't. But I have to try," I croak. "There's no other option. I need to try to save my friends and ensure Zandia is safe."

"How could you even do it?" Mirelle locks eyes with me. "You're not a warrior or a tech expert. How will you disable the entire system?"

"I just need to get into the main lab and get to the control panel. I know exactly which buttons to push on the remote activator, and in the right sequence. I can do a complete wipe of the program. I mean, I know they can redo it. But at least we humans that you saved will no longer be tainted or dangerous to you. Or ourselves."

Mirelle just looks at me.

"I know I can do it." My voice strengthens. "I can prove it. Let me show you." With trembling fingers, I point to her holo tablet. "I can draw the outlay of the planet and the buildings. My brain has it recorded."

My head zaps as I force myself to remember more and more. I've become adept at reading things the chip recorded while I was in training, and now a new memory comes.

"Mirelle! I know the code to disable the motion sensors outside the lab! And I can even remember the passcodes for entry for crafts entering the planet."

"I can cloak. I won't need that. Anyway, they'd be in

contact with any ship and would know I'm not welcome." Her voice is thoughtful, though, and for the first time, I think she is considering doing what I ask. "But having the codes to disable their sensors is critical. Otherwise you'd never be able to get into the building undetected."

I nod, hopeful. "I can do it."

She hands me the tablet. "Show me what you can."

I nod and take a deep breath then begin writing down the things I can recall about the planet alignment, entry protocols, the entire layout of the lab building, and the secret codes needed to type into the entry panels on each lab.

"My memories are getting stronger the more I do this," I murmur, continuing to cipher.

When I'm done, I hand her the tablet. "What do you think? Can you get there safely?"

Mirelle stares at the tablet then at me for a long moment. Finally, she gives a nod. "All right, Sia. I'll take you to Larew."

* * *

Daven

After a sleepless night, I find myself banging on Axe's door.

When he doesn't answer, I pound so hard I crack the metal surface. The pain of it satisfies me.

I draw back my fist to punch the door again when some being catches my arm from behind.

I turn with a snarl to find Axe glowering at me.

He appears even more agitated than I am. "We have to save them," he snarls.

I stop and blink.

167

I expected rebuke from him. He warned me over and over again against trusting these females, yet I chose to mate Sia anyway.

I didn't listen.

Then my heart speeds to a gallop. *"Save them from what?"*

"From termination. Dr. Daneth may attempt surgery, which could kill them or leave them brain dead. We can't let that happen."

I'm running before my brain even comes on line. Axe grabs my arm and swings me in the opposite direction. "They're in the command center discussing it with the king." I accept the redirection, and both of us run toward the building that looms in the distance, the one that Sia admired so many planet rotations ago. "They're waiting for us. You didn't get the summons because you're not wearing your wrist comms."

He's right. I left my domicile without it. It's a wonder I even managed to put on my clothes and boots.

Axe and I ignore the sentries as we stride into the meeting room. It's chilly inside—the thick walls emanating cool even though the morning sun is warm.

Or maybe that's the cold prickling my skin. The fear for Sia.

King Zander doesn't react when we both bow to him before taking our seats.

Seke clears his throat, and the group falls silent. "Now that Axe and Daven have arrived, we can begin. The females are isolated in the dungeon right now, shielded with lead barriers and digital scramblers in case the chips are transmitting. Dr. Daneth can brief us on what he has found.

Dr. Daneth's expression is characteristically impassive.

"I have not detected a signal emanating from Katia's head, incoming or outgoing."

"Can the chip be removed?" King Zander asks.

"It is completely entwined with brain matter. To remove it would mean terminating the patient." Dr. Daneth speaks with no emotion, and I want to twist his head off his neck.

Because Axe is right. They are discussing ending our females' lives to get the chips out.

"My lord," Lon, a Zandian engineer, speaks up. "It seems to me that we should operate on all the rescued females immediately, examine their brains, and remove those chips to learn exactly what we're up against." He looks to the elders in the room, checking for agreement. "I need to examine that technology to find out what is on the chip and how it functions. If the Ocretions are putting chips into humans we owe it to ourselves and our young to learn about it, so we can reverse engineer it and stay safe. Not just for now. For all times."

There are a few non-committal head bobs, but no other Zandian says a word. My heart thuds against my chest, horns stiffen with anger.

Lon continues. "If we must sacrifice one or all of the females to learn about this," he shrugs, "I, for one, believe it's worth the loss."

"No!" I roar it, and I'm on my feet even before I'm aware of standing. "We're not sacrificing the females."

"They may be in on this," Lon says.

"They're not," I growl, and suddenly I'm sure.

I'm certain of Sia. She's not working with her former masters to betray or trick us. She was only protecting her life and the lives of her friends. She was afraid of exactly this outcome–that our king would order their death in the name of security and research.

Compassion for her plight hits me like a fist to the gut. My sweet human might be dissected like a lab beast. I can't allow this to happen.

"They were slaves," Axe growls. "They kept their mouths shut to save their skins. I have no doubt if they had any choice in the matter–which they didn't and don't–their loyalty would lie with Zandia. No doubt."

"Nor do I," I say.

"It might be the only way." Lon rises now too and gets in my face. Only a few inches away, I can feel the heat of his breath and see the anger sparking in his gaze. "Would you have our whole planet compromised? We need to do what's necessary."

"Killing unnecessarily is not our way!" I'm ready to put my hands on him.

"Silence." The king barely raises his voice, but the command makes us all freeze. "Take your seats. We will discuss this rationally."

Lon and I face off for another second before he finally takes a seat. Axe and I lower ourselves, too.

"Dr. Daneth, please continue your investigation and attempt to preserve the life of the human," King Zander says. "If she dies, move forward with autopsy and extraction." He turns his attention to Lon. "Lon, I need you to determine if any recorded information from their chips has actually made it off the planet."

"I think not," Tral, another engineer, speaks up. "I'm in charge of home base comms security, and I haven't seen evidence of any illegal transmissions. Not once, not even when the human Katia had her episode." He touches his holo. "We routinely look to intercept any transmission, anything of interest, and certainly I've had nothing coming from *inside* our planet. Of course we have the usual plethora of random communications from passing freighters and civilians, but nothing outgoing. The humans reported that they felt the recordings activate with certain words..."

"Maybe they have new tech that can hide from your systems." Lon is back on his feet, gesturing. "Maybe we should consider eliminating the risky humans." He looks around. "I'm only voicing what I know other Zandians are thinking."

I'm going to rip his arms off his body. I rise, baring my teeth. Axe is right with me, drawing his sword.

Before I can get to him, King Zander interrupts. "That's enough from you, Lon. Leave the proceedings."

Lon shoots us a dark look as he exits.

Axe and I return it.

King Zander's comms unit beeps, and a holo springs up with one of the dungeon commander's head and shoulders. "My Lord, one of the humans is missing from her cell," the commander says.

"Which one?" King Zander barks.

"Sia. Daven's female."

My female. Yes, Sia *is* my female. My mate. How could I have renounced her? She only did what she had to do to stay alive.

I surge to my feet for a third time.

"How did she escape?" The king's voice is terse. The look he sends me, accusatory.

My heart thunders painfully against my chest, my fists curl at my sides.

"It appears another human sent her free. Mirelle, the pilot."

Master Seke looks up from a communication he received on his wrist comms. "I just had word that the two of them have left the planet."

Chapter Seventeen

*S*ia
    "Brace yourself for hyper drive." Mirelle's voice is calm as she handles controls from the pilot's panel.

Beside her, palms clammy with anxiety, I bob my head. "Yes. All right." The craft is sleek and high tech, and I'm unfamiliar with everything.

There's a strange pulse, like my whole body is falling behind and catching up, and my heart thuds in my chest.

"The first time you experience it awake, it really shocks a human." Mirelle doesn't look at me as her fingers dance over the panel, her eyes focused on the holo displays in front of us.

"We'll be in Larew airspace shortly. Are you ready for this?"

She turns to look at me. Her face is serious. "I can land the craft in a cloaked mode, and they won't see us, Sia. But if you go into that lab, you might not come out alive."

I touch the small laser weapon at my waist. We talked about this on the way to the craft; it was my idea. Mirelle could see I was serious, and I think that was one of the reasons she agreed to do this.

"If I can deactivate the panel, I will. If they are about to capture me, I'll do what needs to be done. I'll notify you so you can save yourself." I swallow hard but my voice is even. "I'm not afraid."

I know how the weapon works. It can vaporize a being, especially at close range. I don't want to think about it, but I'm willing to sacrifice myself for the other humans–and for Zandia.

Mirelle reaches out. "I have faith in you, Sia. You can do this." Her calm voice soothes me.

"I will do my best." My voice is strong now. My confidence is back. "I have to. I owe it to all of you. To Daven. To every being on Zandia."

"You're smarter and stronger than you even know." Mirelle turns back to the panel. "Landing now. Brace again, please."

I lean back into the chair, but I'm not thinking about anything else but the lab, even as the craft touches down with a soft bump.

"I know exactly how to get in and how to do the passcodes," I tell Mirelle. "It's past the hour when any being is here, and the guard won't come back until sun up. I just might succeed."

"They're going to be furious with me for taking you here." Mirelle's voice is low. "But my gut tells me that this is the right thing, Sia. And I've made all of my big decisions based on my gut. It's how I survive. I think my warriors will understand. At least, I hope they will." She grabs my hand. "Be safe."

I nod. "You too. Leave immediately if I'm taken."

Mirelle nods then does a scan of the area via her remote

video ability. We landed behind the grove of trees in front of the lab. Larew is mostly empty; the Ocretions use it for experimentation now, and it's not inhabited except for the colony of overseers and workers.

"This is the best spot," I tell her. "Easy to get to the lab and not near the lava pit."

Mirelle wrinkles her nose. "Why do they even have lava on this planet?"

"It's not really lava. It's an open hole in the ground full of burning gunk. They use it as a garbage incinerator. And to scare slaves. They threaten to toss us in there if we misbehave. They've done it, too."

I try to push back the horrible memories. "But that's behind the building on the other side, and anyway, the lava is all contained in the cement pit."

Mirelle checks her scanners. "You were right. It's quiet, and there are no beings around. I've just used the code you gave me to turn off their motion sensors remotely. Be fast, though." Mirelle squeezes my arm.

She unlocks the craft door and allows me to descend, and I alight onto the grassy ground.

I immediately start walking. When I turn back, I can't see the craft. The cloaking is impeccable! I try not to worry about finding her again because right now my entire focus is on getting into that lab and deactivating these chips.

It's so odd being back here, and more memories rush in. The dormitories, the food hall (so disgusting compared to what we eat on Zandia), the punishments. The lab. The surgery. And most importantly, the main control panel.

I'm a different being than I was when I lived here. The short time on Zandia–my time with Daven–has utterly changed me.

I know so much more is possible than I did when I was

here. I've seen something worth living for. Something worth fighting for. I've seen humans in important roles–like Mirelle. I've seen humans happily mated with families. The strength of those humans has seeped into my veins.

The grass is soft and a little dewy under my feet–that's a new experience. I never was allowed to walk around at night. Apart from that, everything looks and feels the same. As I approach the main lab building, my shoes a little damp, my heart races. Every fiber of my being wants to run back to the safety of Mirelle's craft and get far away from here.

But I need to do this.

I glance around, smelling the familiar odor of the acrid cleanser they use on the building, even the outside. There are also faint wisps of the aroma of the burning rubbage in the far off lava pit brought to me on the small breeze that whispers past. That scent never failed to terrify us–but I push that thought away.

There are no beings anywhere in sight. I raise a hand, hesitate, and type in the code to enter the lab. "77477564," I whisper to myself. "My old master's personal code."

There's a brief pause when nothing happens, and my stomach roils, wondering if the codes were changed. *Of course they were; how could I be so stupid?* Then the door glides open without a sound, and I step inside.

I did it. I'm here.

At first, I double over and almost vomit. Weak in the knees, I can barely stand. The smell of antiseptic floods my nose, and memories of my surgeries, the pain, the terror, overwhelm me.

I stumble and fall against a nearby wall. Stars, I can't do this.

I feel small again. Insignificant. Afraid for my life.

But then I think of Daven. I touch the crystal he embedded in my ear.

I'm not helpless. I'm not a slave here anymore.

I have a chance to live.

And I need to make sure I get it. I need to make sure Katia, Flora, Alyza and Janae get theirs.

I force myself to stand and shake my arms and then my legs to control the jitters. "There's no going back now," I mouth silently. I know better than to speak aloud, even in my panic–the motion sensors are off, but I can't make a sound. Who knows if any being is listening? "I can do this."

The main lights are off, but the night lights are on, and I know the way, anyway. I was marched along this very path to my operations every planet rotation.

My feet slip a little as I walk, and I steady myself. That dew from the grass affected my shoes more than I realized.

I make it down the first hallway, enter the new pass-code. The door glides open, as if beckoning me in.

And there it is, at the end of the room–the main control panel. My goal is in sight!

Can it possibly be this easy?

I hurry over to the panel.

The buttons are backlit in pale green, and the holo entry screen flashes blue. My master entered the code several times, and I remember it perfectly.

"Enter the emergency code," I tell myself and try to steady my fingers. "One wrong try, and it sets off the alarm."

I take a deep breath and then enter the code, the one I'm not supposed to know. The one no slave should know. The one I only have in my mind because the very tech they installed in our heads allowed us to record things while they were working on us.

There's a soft beep, and the screen lights up. "Emergency Protocol Activated. Are you sure you want to proceed? Continuation can mean the deactivation of the entire Project Alpha Protocol."

I hit "Yes. Proceed."

The next choice: "Individual Deactivation or Entire Project?"

I select "Entire Project."

The options array on the holo in front of me: *Deactivate All Alpha One Slaves* or *Exterminate All Alpha One Slaves*.

I immediately press *Deactivate All.*

There's a beep and a hum. The lights in the room come up suddenly, and an alarm blares.

Stars! What's happening?

Another command shows up on the screen.

"Verify Deactivate All on remote device."

Stars. Remote device? This is definitely new. They never had that before!

Panicked, I glance around the room. Where and what is the remote device I need? Everything was supposed to be right here on this panel! They've changed it up.

I'm not going to succeed.

There's the sound of voices shouting, and footsteps, and suddenly two guards burst into the room.

"Halt!"

They have weapons raised, trained at me.

Unable to move, I stand and stare.

"It's a slave!"

"How did she even get in here?"

"Seize her. Take her to the commander."

Strong arms grab me, twisting hard, and I scream in pain.

Before they can move me, though, a familiar voice cuts through the room.

"Which one is it? Is it a missing Alpha?"

It's my old master.

"Release her," he commands the guards. "Let me see her face. I need to be sure."

He grabs my chin with his warty hand. "You look different." He stares at me. "But it's you. Sia. Where were you? Who took you? We thought you were all dead."

I don't answer.

He stands in front of me. "You're back, and you managed somehow to get into the panel?" He's irritated and surprised. "But it's no good, as you can see. Because you also need to verify the commands on here." He pats a device at his waist. "I decided to make things more secure, after we lost your batch, you see."

He steps closer. "This isn't exactly a shame, though. In fact, it's a bonus. You must have been somewhere quite interesting. Perhaps with some Zandians? I can't wait to extract that chip and find out what you've heard and seen." His voice rises with glee. "We'll do it immediately. Take her to the med bay."

It's over. If they get to the chip, I'm not only dead, but I've jeopardized the entire planet of Zandia and everyone I care about. I can't let that happen. I don't know what my chip recorded before I figured out how to make it stop, and even a single vision or piece of information could be enough to enrage the Ocretions enough to have them attack Zandia.

I need to do something. I need to fix this. Finish it.

Before they can take me, I move. I grab the gun from under my tunic and aim at the first guard. Pull the trigger.

He falls to the floor, hard, head bounding and blood spattering, and I aim at the second one before I can think. I get him, too, but the shock of it is so startling that I drop my gun. Stars!

My master roars and grabs his own weapon, but he's not a guard, he's a scientist. His reflexes are slow. As he moves toward me, he slips a little on the viscous blood trail from the dead guards.

It provides the moment I need, and I take it. I grab at the device at his waist, pull it into my hand, turn and run.

If I can just get back to Mirelle, I'll be safe. We'll all be safe!

I make it out of the building, slipping wildly, not sure if it's the residual dew or the guards' blood or both that has me careening into walls and sliding.

But the craft is too far, and my master is already behind me, screaming my name.

"Sia!" He howls, and I feel a blast of laser rush past my skin, the heat singing my cheek. He missed—but next time he won't. If he gets me, that means he gets my chip.

"Give it up!" he shouts. "If you stop now, I won't torture you before I kill you."

He blasts again, and this time it catches the side of my leg. The searing burn is overwhelming, and my whole brain goes blank with static as I try to stay on my feet—but I can't.

I scream in pain and panic, stumble, and fall. He's nearly on top of me.

I manage to get up and keep running, but my lungs burn, and my body is slow. I can feel myself bleeding, know I'm probably going into shock soon. And it's clear I can never escape him. If I'd just been able to hold onto that weapon! But I didn't.

I need help.

But no. Help won't come. Mirelle said she won't leave the craft, and I know she's a human who keeps her word. I wouldn't want her to endanger herself.

I'm alone here. I need to make a decision.

The smell of the lava pit hits my nostrils, and I see the eerie orange glow of its fire, sending out trickles of sick light into the dark.

I race towards the pit, and as I do, the device in my hand beeps.

"Confirm deactivate all," a voice intones. "Press YES to deactivate all."

But I can't do anything but run and try to dodge the laser blasts.

"Confirm deactivate all," the device repeats. "If confirmation is not given in five seconds, command will be rejected."

Stars! I need to do this.

The smell of burning matter grows stronger, and I skid to a halt—I'm at the edge of the pit.

"Sia!" My old master is close behind. "Give that to me. Immediately."

There's panic in his voice. Why is he not shooting me?

Oh!

I understand. If he does, I'll fall into the pit, taking with me the device...and my brain. The two things he needs.

"Stop!" I scream, holding up the device. "Or I'll jump."

Everything slows to a crawl.

Time seems to undulate in front of me.

My time is nearly up, but it feels like I have all of it in my hands.

With shaking fingers, I press the flashing button, *Deactive All.*

There's a strange whirring sensation in my head, and then...nothing. As if the chip has truly stopped working.

But can my master still get images and recordings from it anyway? I don't exactly know if "Deactivate All" means completely shut down and wipe old memories or just shut down.

I can't take the chance.

I look backwards then into the pit.

There's only one way to be sure that I can keep Daven safe–and Mirelle–and all of the beings on Zandia.

I take a deep breath.

* * *

Daven

"Faster!" I urge, as Axe gently guides our cloaked craft to touch down next to Mirelle's. She's cloaked from enemies, but not from us. When she sent us an emergency signal a short time ago, we were already on the way to Larew. She had previously relayed a message saying where they were going and what Sia was going to do and had requested backup.

I open the communication tab but before I can speak, Domm, one of Mirelle's masters and mates exclaims, "Mirelle, what the *veck* were you thinking?" He and Lanz, her other mate and master, came along on the flight to make sure their human was safe.

Our holo screen shows the outline of her craft behind the grove of trees, and our scanners show us the layout of the planet–mostly buildings. I'm frantic for Sia, but I don't see beings anywhere in our vicinity.

Mirelle's voice is even and clear over our comms. "I was thinking that I could help save more humans. Maybe even Zandia. But Sia's in trouble, Daven. I heard her through the comms for a while, but her receiver must have fallen out. She was being chased and may be caught. I should tell you..." she trails off.

My heart thuds painfully against my chest.

"She intends to sacrifice herself if the need arises."

"No!" The word rips from my throat. "I won't let that happen. Axe, we have to find her."

"I know," Mirelle says. "I wanted to help her, but I couldn't risk leaving my craft."

"*Vecking* straight you couldn't," Lanz mutters, already jogging toward Sia's craft. Domm is right behind him.

Axe and I grab our weapons and race from the craft, as well. I'm unfamiliar with the layout of the planet, but once we approach the buildings, I hear voices.

Mirelle speaks to us through the comms unit. "I've turned off all their sensors and cameras using the codes Sia remembered, and I can guide you. Go left, then right twenty paces to the flat gray building. I think they're behind it. Hurry."

We rush, but once we arrive at the location Mirelle told us, we slow our pace and peer out from behind the corner of a flat gray structure that looks like a dormitory.

In the distance, not too far, there's an orange-yellow glow, and I detect heat. *Veck,* is that a huge fire pit?

To my horror, there's a small figure right at the edge.

Sia!

She's bloody and appears weak, and she's holding something in her hand, some piece of tech.

An Ocretion stands a few feet from her, weapon pointed, but he's not using it. Instead, he pleads as he inches closer. "Listen, Sia, you're smart. Give me the device, and we'll promote you. You won't work in the labs anymore. You can choose! Ag worker, pleasure slave? Your choice. You can even bring a friend."

Ocretions aren't known for their sympathy or their flair, and he's clearly lying. His voice doesn't even have a trace of honey in it, not that she'd believe it, anyway. My Sia is too smart for that.

For a split second, my memory flashes back to my first human, the one who betrayed me. But this is different. I know Sia isn't like that. She isn't here to betray us Zandians. She didn't ask me to follow her. Whatever she's doing, she's trying to help.

"Do you want a bigger dorm? We won't use the shock stick on you again, I promise." He reaches out a hand.

"Stay away!" Sia's voice is strong. "I'll drop it, I swear." She's bleeding and swaying. I'm terrified that she'll just fall forward into the fire, she seems so unsteady as she holds her arm out, dangling the device in her fingers over the fire.

"I'm your master, Sia. Surely the loyalty we built into you is still there. This is a direct command. Come to me now and hand me the device." He's snarling now, nearly close enough to grab her. He'll try anything to get his prize.

"Never. I'll never let you get my chip." She stares him down. "I'd rather die."

He steps even closer and reaches for her.

She looks at him, then down at the pit, and I know what she's going to do. She's going to sacrifice herself, so he can't get to her chip.

"No!" I yell at the top of my lungs.

Startled, they both turn, and I line up to take my shot. With perfect aim, I can blast my laser weapon through her old master's heart then his head.

But I don't need to. Sia reaches out and gives her old master a hard shove, and he teeters and shouts at the edge of the pit.

Sia has enough sense to jump back as his body swings and careens, seemingly taking forever, then topples forward into the pit.

Flames flare as they engulf his body, then there's silence.

I race to Sia and snatch her into my arms. Just the feel of her small, fragile body against mine makes me want to fall to my knees in thanks.

"Sia! You're safe. You're all right." I can barely believe it.

"Daven," she says with wonder.

I pull her further from the edge of the horrific hole. "Come, we need to get back to the craft immediately."

Axe has his back to me, weapon up, looking for any other guards. It's oddly silent, until I hear muted yells in the distance. "We need to get the *veck* out of here," Axe growls. "Before any other being sees us."

I lift Sia, and the feeling of deja vu flickers. This is almost how we started. Except this time she means more to me than I could have ever known.

"Daven, what are you doing here?" Sia's voice cracks, but I can't answer yet. First we need to get back to our ship.

It doesn't take long before we're safely ensconced inside the craft. I communicate with Mirelle. "Package retrieved. Depart immediately."

"On it, you first," she replies, and Axe starts up the craft.

Within moments, we lift off the ground, and then we hurtle through the stars, away from Larew, where we've left at least one Ocretion dead and a mystery that they're not going to like once they investigate. But the only Ocretion who saw Zandians, Sia's old master, is dead. Mirelle remotely turned off their sensors and cameras, so ideally they'll have no true idea about who came in and ruined their lab, even if they have suspicions. But I can't focus right now on how to handle that. All I care about is Sia.

I cradle Sia in my lap, unwilling to even set her down. I apply healing patches to the wound on her leg, which–thank *veck*–seems superficial. I give her fluid.

"Daven." Her forehead wrinkles with concern. She searches my face.

"Shh, little human. You're safe. We're headed back to Zandia. Your home."

She relaxes in my arms, leaning her head against my shoulder.

"What happened back there, Sia?"

She blinks, then she gives me a small smile. "I did it. I did what I came to do."

"Which was what?" I wipe her brow, removing flecks of blood and sweat. "Why would you go to Larew? This is where you were enslaved. What were you thinking?"

"I got information from my chip, Daven. I remembered how to undo the whole Alpha project! And I did it."

Mirelle had told me as much, but I like hearing it from Sia. Seeing my brave little mate's pride. "How, my sweet female?"

"I deactivated all of us Alpha Project slaves, and our chips are completely inactive now. We're safe, and so is Zandia. We won't bring harm to you, not ever."

I clutch her to my chest. "Why didn't you tell us that you could do that?"

"I only figured it out this planet rotation. When I was in the cell, I remembered. I knew you'd never believe me. Nor would Seke. Nor the king. Not after I lied about so much for so long."

She's not wrong. Anything she said after she was imprisoned would have been taken with severe suspicion. And they'd have sacrificed some or all of the humans, probably, instead of trying to deactivate them, especially if Marx had anything to say about it.

She explains to me how she remembered all of the information from the chip and how she drew out layouts and codes for Mirelle and convinced Mirelle to fly her to Larew. How Mirelle approved the plan because she felt it was right in her gut, and her gut is never wrong.

She adds, "And then the one human capable of helping me happened to visit me in my cell. I explained the situation to Mirelle, and she was willing to fly me to Larew. Please don't punish her. It was all my idea. I know it seems crazy, but I had a plan. I was going to eliminate myself if there was any chance they'd catch me."

My heart pounds, and I can't speak. My sweet human planned to eliminate herself. I could have lost her—not just to the Ocretions but by her own choosing.

The idea slays me.

"I would have tossed myself in that pit rather than let him get the chip. I wouldn't let them get it or me if there was any chance that there was information about Zandia on it."

Veck.

"I saw that." There's a tremor in my voice. Now I understand what it means to be changed by a human. To feel emotions. To love. "I'm glad you didn't," I choke. The words completely fail to communicate the depth of the horror I felt when I thought I'd lose her forever.

She continues, "And I have his remote device. Your engineers can study it to learn more about what they've created." She's still clutching something in her hand, and she gives it to me. It's slick with blood and sweat, so I take it and hand it to Axe; let him deal with it.

"They'll rebuild, better and stronger, but at least you'll

know what they're doing. We can stay a step ahead. Or you can," she falters.

I take her face in my hands. "We can."

"Am I going back to prison? Or...will I be sent away?"

"No," I say. "That won't happen."

It's not my place to make such a promise, but I will die before I allow any being to harm Sia. If King Zander sends her away, I will go, too. And she's definitely not going to be dissected, that much is for sure.

"Daven, I'm so sorry for everything. For the lies. That I didn't tell you about the chip from the beginning. I hope you understand that I felt I had no choice. I felt like if I told you, I'd die. But I made it right. I deactivated them all, so we can't harm you. Even if your king decides to... get rid of us," she shudders, "at least I fixed my mistake."

I run my knuckles down her cheek. Kiss her dark hair. "You did, sweet human. I'm sorry, too. I shouldn't have believed you would betray us. I felt you wouldn't, but the enormity of what you revealed punched me in the gut."

She reaches up and touches my face, her small palm curving around my cheek. "It happened before to you," she says softly. "I know that. I never wanted to hurt you like that again, but I know I did. I shared with you everything I felt I could and still stay alive. It was a horrible line to walk."

I shake my head. "I understand why you held back the whole truth. Your lives depended on your secret. I could never fault you for that." I lift her chin and brush my lips softly across hers. "I love you, sweet human. I don't ever want to lose you again."

Tears fill her eyes. "Does that mean I'm still yours?"

I kiss her again, harder this time. A claiming kiss. The kind to make her remember she belongs to me fully.

She responds, looping one slender arm around my neck, the other hand lifting to grasp one of my horns.

My cock and horn instantly go rock hard.

"That's right, Sia." There's a growl in my voice now. "You're mine. My mate to master. My mate to breed. My mate to demand complete obedience." I drag my open mouth down the side of her neck, then give her a gentle nip.

"Mmm." She makes a happy sound.

"And don't think there won't be consequences for risking your life." I put enough heat into my threat to make her moan. "That sweet ass of yours will be sore for days." I cup her breast and squeeze. "But I promise you'll love every minute of it."

Chapter Eighteen

Sia

S I lived my entire life on Larew, yet returning to Zandia feels like coming home. Especially with Daven clasping my hand in his. Sweeping me up into his arms before he carries me across the threshold of our domicile.

Axe offered to handle the debrief when we landed, so Daven could take me straight home.

Because I do have a home now. It's with Daven. On this beautiful planet, with these brave and honorable beings—both Zandian and human alike.

Tears leak from my eyes at the beauty of it.

Daven goes still when he scents them. "Are you afraid of your punishment, little one?"

I smile and shake my head. "No, Master. I'm happy."

His brow furrows. "You're happy, so you cry?"

I give a watery laugh. "Yes. It's a release of emotions. Humans sometimes cry when they are happy."

His brow smooths, and he strides to the washtube on long legs. "Do I make you happy, sweet girl?"

"Yes, Master."

"How happy?"

He sets me on my feet outside the washtube and tugs off my bloodied gown then removes his own tunic and leggings.

"This happy." I loop my arms around his neck to pull his head down, stand on my tiptoes and lift my face to his."

He walks me backward into the washtube as our lips collide. The door swishes closed, and water begins to fill the tube, but I barely notice it because Daven is giving me the kiss of a lifetime. It's passionate and hard, like the cock straining against my ribcage.

He tucks a forearm under my ass and boosts me up to wrap my legs around his waist. Presses me against the washtube wall to slide his tongue between my lips. I moan into his mouth. More when his cock finds the notch between my legs.

The contact of his smooth skin against my most sensitive parts makes me greedy for more.

"Please, Master," I whimper.

"You want this?" he growls, rubbing the large head of his cock against my entrance.

"Yes, please."

He thrusts in, making me gasp with pleasure. With the intensity of it.

"Thank you, Master." I almost want to weep with joy again. I love this feeling—not just the physical pleasure, but what it means. My Master enjoying himself with me. Claiming me as his mate. Perhaps even breeding me.

"You don't have to thank me, little one." Daven pins me against the wall and thrusts, fingers splayed across my ass to hold me in position. "This is for my pleasure. And *vecking* you will become my duty—for Zandia."

I'm breathless. Hot. The water is up to our waists now, engulfing us. "For Zandia?" I pant, confused.

The water rises to my breasts, then my shoulders.

"That's right." Daven grins at me. "For repopulation of our planet."

The water is up to my chin. When I smile back, it enters my mouth, and I have to close it quickly as I squeeze my eyes shut for complete immersion.

He *does* mean to put young in me. We will be a family, like that sweet family I met outside the clinic.

Joy comes on so hard I think I might burst. When the water begins to rapidly drain, I'm laughing. Crying. Bucking against Daven with my first climax.

He growls when my muscles clamp around his cock. The moment the water has drained below our waist, he begins to pound into me with punishing strokes.

The water on our skin makes the slide all the more glorious and as the warm air blows across it to dry us, Daven roars out his release.

"Yes, please," I babble, gratitude at the wonder of all my life has become, humbling me. "Thank you, Master. Thank you."

Daven leans his head against mine. "You please me, little one. So much."

"Thank you, Master," I whisper again. "I'm so happy I'm yours."

"You are mine. Forever, Sia. I won't let anything happen to you or your friends. No matter what," he promises.

Of course, I understand him. Our fates have not yet been decided. We are all subject to the king here.

But knowing Daven will protect me keeps all anxiety at bay. I have a master now. A mate. That's all that matters to me.

* * *

Daven

"It's time for your punishment, little one."

I've tended to Sia's wounds and fed her. Axe let me know that the debriefing went well. Katia recovered as soon as the chips were deactivated.

Mirelle, Lanz and Domm returned safely and were debriefed. I have to assume the two warriors are also lovingly taking their female to task right now.

I'm satisfied that Sia appears aroused and alert but not particularly afraid. She trusts me. She likes to submit to me—just as it should be.

This is the reason humans are so compatible with our species, I presume. This sexual bonding makes relations so intensely satisfying for both species. The same weakness that made humans ideal for enslavement by the Ocretions makes them absolutely perfect citizens of Zandia.

Once bonded, they are fiercely loyal. Endlessly giving. Perfectly aligned with the good of the planet.

At least that's how I see it now.

Before Sia, I wasn't so sure. Especially after Illiana.

But she's shown me what the other mated Zandians have sworn to be true—human females were made for us.

I stand her in front of me. She clasps her hands in front of her and lowers her gaze.

"No, look at me." I separate her hands, so I can see her pretty pussy.

She lifts her chin to gaze into my eyes.

"Beautiful female," I purr, stroking one palm down her arm as the other slides over her hip.

I scent her arousal almost immediately, a heady perfume that makes my horns thicken and pulse.

"You're going to be punished for putting your life at risk on Larew."

"Yes, Master," she whispers, sweet as honey.

I stand and pull a large, square, padded footrest to the center of the room. "Straddle this and lie down," I command.

She obeys, presenting a perfect, beautiful target for my hand. Her buttocks are spread apart at the end of the stool. Her tits press against the opposite end, so her head hangs off.

I slap my hand down on one side of her ass.

She gasps, but holds still.

I watch as my handprint blooms on her olive skin.

I give her other cheek the same treatment then begin her spanking in earnest, alternating right and left until she's gasping and whimpering.

"Good girl," I murmur. "You're taking your punishment so well."

"Thank you, Master," she whimpers.

I stand back to admire my handiwork. Her ass has taken on a rosy glow. I'm torn between using the strap or *vecking* her pretty ass. It looks far too inviting in this position to pass by the opportunity.

I settle for a brief strapping before her ass-vecking.

"Put your legs together and slide forward so your hands touch the floor," I instruct.

I'm satisfied when she obeys without complaint.

I pick up the strap. "I'm going to give you ten stripes, and then I'm going to show you where you get *vecked* when you've been naughty."

She makes an unintelligible sound.

I bring the strap down with a snap, right across the middle of her buttocks.

She squeals.

I rub away the sting, then deliver another stroke. "Are you going to put yourself at risk again, little human?"

"No, Master!" she cries, kicking up one foot.

I give her three more strokes. "We're halfway through." I stop to rub again. "You're taking it so well."

"Thank you, Master." She sounds a little pouty, but I find it adorable.

I deliver the last five strokes with slow, even precision, striping down to where thigh meets buttock then back up again to the center of her ass. "Good girl," I praise when we're finished. "Now move back to the previous position."

As she complies, I get a lubricant. I release a dollop between her cheeks, then massage it into the rosebud of her anus. I go slowly, prying her open with my finger, making her moan with pleasure.

"Do you like when I take your ass, pretty human?"

"Um..."

"Hmm?"

She doesn't answer. I laugh. "Is that a no, but you don't want to tell me? Or is it a mixture of yes and no?"

"A mixture of yes and no," she admits.

I pump my finger in and out of her ass. "I'll teach you to like it, sweet girl. Even when it's punishment, you should feel the pleasure."

She moans.

I remove my finger and slide off my leggings, rubbing more lubricant liberally over my cock.

"Reach back and hold your cheeks wide for me, naughty human," I tell her.

I've never seen anything so erotic or beautiful as my sweet mate obeying my command. I have to force myself to go slowly, to rub between her legs to make sure she's slick and wet there first.

"Use your fingers," I tell her, lining the head of my cock up with her back pucker. "Rub this sweet little pussy while I *veck* your ass."

She releases her ass cheeks and slides her hand under her hips as I apply gentle pressure to breech her anus.

A shudder of pleasure runs through me at the sensation of claiming her tight ass. I go slowly, pressing in and out with even strokes as she works her fingers between her legs.

When she begins to mewl and moan with more intensity, I pick up my speed, surrendering to my lust. The room spins, and I somehow seem to sense every crystal on Zandia—all of its energy pulsing with me, for me.

"Daven, I need to come!" She's full of urgency.

My first inclination is to say "Veck, yes, come." but this is still a punishment, after all - I'll make her wait.

"No," I growl, barely able to talk through my anticipation. "You hold it, my sweet little human. Not yet for you."

She cries out in frustration, and the sound of her voice pushes me over the edge.

My balls draw up and pump, and then I come with a roar, burying myself deep in her ass to fill her with my rainbow essence. I grab her hips and pull her to me hard as my cock throbs, pushing into her as deeply as I can.

When I'm exhausted, I tap her shoulder. "Squeeze your ass cheeks together, Sia. Make sure every drop of my cum stays in that naughty ass while I pull out."

She moans. "Daven, I need to come."

I reach back and slap her buttocks once. "Remember the rules. You come when I say."

"Yes, Master," she whispers. I feel her clench around my cock, and *veck,* if I'm not ready to harden another time.

"Oooh," she murmurs as I slowly draw my cock out.

"It might sting a little," I warn her. "Because your ass is so well used right now."

It probably won't sting at all, and if it does, it will fade. And after all, I'm going to reward her for waiting so nicely with a great orgasm.

She fidgets below me as I pull my cock out inch by inch. "Keep squeezing me," I warn her.

She obeys, keeping her ass muscles nice and tight.

I watch and listen for signs that it's too much, but the only noises she makes are ones of pleasure.

When I'm completely out of her body, I relax. "*Veck*," I murmur. "This is how I like to see you. All naked and laid out, with your pretty ass full of my cum."

"Yes, Master," is all she says, but I can scent her arousal growing stronger by the minute.

"You can let go now." I stroke her skin.

She relaxes her body and a little rainbow cum trickles out of her pretty rosebud.

Now it's definite–I'm turned on and ready to go again.

"I'm going to have to punish you that way more often," I murmur. "Maybe next time I'll put in a little plug to make sure my cum stays in there longer. Make you walk around with it until I'm ready to come again."

I think she likes that idea because even though she says, "nooo," she wiggles and writhes.

I smile and stroke her ass, thinking of all the ways we can pleasure each other in the future.

"Is it my turn?" She flips over and reaches up to give me a kiss. Her arms twine around my horns. "You can *veck* my ass any time you want if you please, please just let me come!"

"Almost." I flop down to relax for a minute, thinking of

how best to give her pleasure. Her hands on my horns is driving me to distraction–and I love it. I won't stop her from doing this if she likes it too.

"Keep doing that. Stroke them harder than you would my cock. Grab them with your fists, Sia." My voice is deep with need.

She does, her motions tentative at first. But when she gets into a rhythm and I start to groan in pleasure, she works her hands harder, gaining confidence.

"Yeah baby, like that. Keep going." My body starts to thrum with desire, even more than before. having the human touch me in such an intimate way is the best thing I've ever felt.

I stroke her soft skin, her breasts, then pinch a nipple. My cock hardens as do my horns, and the double pleasure makes me almost giddy with the need to come again. I feel like I'm harder than I've ever been before.

But I want to reward her for her obedience before I take my pleasure, so I pull her hands away softly, even though I vecking love the sensation. "Lie down on the platform, and spread your legs, sweetling. I think you'll like this."

She obeys instantly. "Daven, please." Her voice is full of desire.

"Please what? Put my tongue into that pussy?"

"Yes, yes, there right...aaaah. Oh!" She cries out as I flick my tongue against her clit, then thrust it into her delicious essence. "Daven, oh stars, I'm going to come already."

"Not yet. When I say," I order although I don't know if either of us can actually wait that much longer.

I lick her slowly, flick my tongue around her clit so fast it almost vibrates. When she's moaning and writhing, I grab her thighs, pull them father apart to get my head in as closely as I can, and fuck her with my tongue. My horns are right up against her skin and the pressure of her body rubbing on them adds to my desire. It's almost too much.

She's dripping wet, and I can't get enough of her flavor. My Sia. Mine.

I can make her come on my tongue, but I want my cock in her pussy again.

"Just a few more minutes," I promise her, straddling her body. "Look at me, Sia."

We gaze into each other's eyes as I hover over her, the smell of our sex in the air, and it feels like I'm looking into her soul. My soul. A magical combination of the best of us.

I slide my cock into her pussy, not looking away from her face.

"Come for me," I whisper. "Make it the best one you've ever had."

I begin to thrust, gently, then harder. "Whenever you're ready," I tell her, "I'll come too."

Our bodies are slick with sweat and sex, and before long her eyes shut, and she begins to make a high keening noise. Then she clenches her pussy around my cock and screams out her pleasure, and that's all it takes to send me over the edge again. I pump again and again, both of us coming together, until my bliss sends me nearly to the edge of the universe.

"Sweet human," I croon when I'm through. I ease out and lift her from the bed, carrying her once more to the washtube.

She's limp from her release, so I hold her as we clean our bodies a second time then carry her to our sleeping platform.

She is so precious to me. I never before understood how Zandians could bond so tightly to their human mates, but now it's engrained in my brain. This little being is every-thing to me.

I only hope she feels the same way.

She turns into me, placing her hand on my chest. "I love you, Daven," she murmurs.

The words pierce me straight through the heart.

Love.

My mate loves me. It's a human concept, but one many here have come to understand.

And now, I realize, so have I.

This beautiful female has utterly changed me. I'm as bonded to her as she is to me. She's shown me what it is to trust again. To care. And yes, to love.

I cradle the side of her face and kiss her deeply. "I love you, Sia. My sweet mate."

Epilogue

Sia

      I lie back on Dr. Daneth's table as a tiny winged device flies over and around my swelling belly

A holograph of our baby springs into the air above us.

Daven's hand tightens over mine. "It's a male."

Does his voice sound choked?

I think it does.

Daven is as excited for this young as I am.

We're still just learning about one another. Every planet rotation, I fall more deeply in love with this male.

He's more than I ever dreamed possible. I never knew males like him existed. But here he is—strong and handsome. Protective. Caring. Loving.

He will make the perfect father to our young.

After my trip to Larew, I was called before the king to answer for my crimes.

Daven told me to be completely honest about everything. I was, I finally felt I had nothing to fear, and I counseled my friends to do the same. After meeting with each of us individually and then with our assigned masters, King

Zander decreed we could stay on Zandia, so long as we were each mated to a Zandian, and our mates had complete confidence in us.

I was the only one from our group in that situation at the time, so the rest were put on probation, but Daven believes they will eventually all be accepted here.

The insect-like tech continues to circle my abdomen as Bayla records voice-notes on a tablet.

"Wait," Daven says, a note of alarm in his voice. "What is that?"

I peer at the holo. He's right, our baby looks deformed.

I sit up, my hands flying to my belly.

Bayla does not seem alarmed, though. In fact, she is smiling.

She uses her fingertips to rotate the holo. "That," she says, enlarging the holo, "is a second baby. And it looks to me like it's a girl."

"Oh, sweet mother Earth!" I exclaim. "Twins?"

"Yes," Bayla laughs. "It appears you are having twins."

Daven chokes out a laugh and scoops me into his arms.

"Hold on," Bayla chides with a smile, but Daven is spinning me around and kissing me all over.

"Twins! I can't believe it!" Daven says. "Two for one! We get to grow our family doubly fast. I'm so happy."

I laugh, soaking up his joy, his love, his kisses. This moment.

Everything my life has become.

It is so beyond what I ever imagined possible. Sometimes I'm so happy I ache with joy.

* * *

Thank you for reading *Rescued by the Zandian*. If you enjoyed it, **we would so appreciate your review.** They make a huge difference for indie authors. Be sure to sign up for Renee's newsletter to get word of the next Zandian Bride release, as well as sales and bonus content.

Want FREE books?

Read all the Zandian Brides Series

Night of the Zandians
    Bought by the Zandians
    Mastered by the Zandians
    Zandian Lights
    Kept by the Zandian
    Claimed by the Zandian
    Stolen by the Zandian
    Rescued by the Zandian

Other Titles by Renee Rose

Paranormal

Wolf Ridge High Series

Alpha Bully

Alpha Knight

Step Alpha

Two Marks Series

Untamed

Tempted

Desired

Enticed

Wolf Ranch Series

Rough

Wild

Feral

Savage

Fierce

Ruthless

Bad Boy Alphas Series

Alpha's Temptation

Alpha's Danger

Alpha's Prize

Alpha's Challenge

Alpha's Obsession

Alpha's Desire

Alpha's War

Alpha's Mission

Alpha's Bane

Alpha's Secret

Alpha's Prey

Alpha's Sun

Shifter Ops

Alpha's Moon

Alpha's Vow

Alpha's Revenge

Alpha's Fire

Alpha's Rescue

Alpha's Command

Midnight Doms

Alpha's Blood

His Captive Mortal

All Souls Night

Alpha Doms Series

The Alpha's Hunger

The Alpha's Promise

The Alpha's Punishment

The Alpha's Protection (Dirty Daddies)

Other Paranormal

The Winter Storm: An Ever After Chronicle

Made Men Series

Don't Tease Me

Don't Tempt Me

Don't Make Me

Chicago Bratva

"Prelude" in Black Light: Roulette War

The Director

The Fixer

"Owned" in Black Light: Roulette Rematch

The Enforcer

The Soldier

The Hacker

The Bookie

The Cleaner

The Player

The Gatekeeper

Alpha Mountain

Hero

Rebel

Warrior

Vegas Underground Mafia Romance

King of Diamonds

Mafia Daddy

Jack of Spades

Ace of Hearts

Joker's Wild

His Queen of Clubs

Dead Man's Hand

Wild Card

Contemporary

Daddy Rules Series

Fire Daddy

Hollywood Daddy

Stepbrother Daddy

Master Me Series

Her Royal Master

Her Russian Master

Her Marine Master

Yes, Doctor

Double Doms Series

Theirs to Punish

Theirs to Protect

Holiday Feel-Good

Scoring with Santa

Saved

Other Contemporary

Black Light: Valentine Roulette

Black Light: Roulette Redux

Black Light: Celebrity Roulette

Black Light: Roulette War

Black Light: Roulette Rematch

Punishing Portia (written as Darling Adams)

The Professor's Girl

Safe in his Arms

Sci-Fi

Zandian Masters Series

His Human Slave

His Human Prisoner

Training His Human

His Human Rebel

His Human Vessel

His Mate and Master

Zandian Pet

Their Zandian Mate

His Human Possession

Zandian Brides

Night of the Zandians

Bought by the Zandians

Mastered by the Zandians

Zandian Lights

Kept by the Zandian

Claimed by the Zandian

Stolen by the Zandian

Other Sci-Fi

The Hand of Vengeance

Her Alien Masters

Also by Rebel West / Alexis Alvarez

Read More by Rebel West / Alexis Alvarez

Zandian Brides Series (with co-writer Renee Rose)

Night of the Zandians

Bought by the Zandians

Mastered by the Zandians

Zandian Lights

Kept by the Zandian

Claimed by the Zandian

Stolen by the Zandian

Rescued by the Zandian

Sci-Fi Romance

Conquered by the Alien Prince: Luminar Masters, Book 1

Steamy, Contemporary Romance

Perfect Match

A Handful of Fire

Boston

Dream Girl

Kinky/BDSM Romance

His Firm Direction

Casey's Choice

Capturing Kate

Myka and the Millionaire

Return

About Renee Rose

USA TODAY BESTSELLING AUTHOR RENEE ROSE loves a dominant, dirty-talking alpha hero! She's sold over a half million copies of steamy romance with varying levels of kink. Her books have been featured in USA Today's *Happily Ever After* and *Popsugar*. Named Eroticon USA's Next Top Erotic Author in 2013, she has also won *Spunky and Sassy's* Favorite Sci-Fi and Anthology author, and *The Romance Reviews* Best Historical Romance. She's hit the *USA Today* list seven times with her Wolf Ranch books and various anthologies.

Please follow her on:
   Bookbub | Goodreads | Instagram

Renee loves to connect with readers!
www.reneeroseromance.com
reneeroseauthor@gmail.com

About Rebel West

Rebel West writes hot sci-fi with aliens so sexy you'll swoon! She's into photography and travel, and when she's not figuring out ways to get her main characters together, she's out with her camera looking for inspiration. Find her under her other pen name, Alexis Alvarez, where she writes contemporary romance and kinky/spanky/BDSM books.

Read More by Rebel West / Alexis Alvarez

Sci-Fi Romance

Conquered by the Alien Prince: Luminar Masters, Book 1

Steamy, Contemporary Romance:

Perfect Match
A Handful of Fire
Boston
Dream Girl

Kinky/BDSM Romance:
Hammered
His Firm Direction
Casey's Choice
Capturing Kate
Myka and the Millionaire
Return
Her Vampire Temptation

Newsletter: https://goo.gl/forms/iVRhZbk2somz8v6h2
Website: http://graffitifiction.com/
Amazon Author Page: https://www.amazon.com/Alexis-Alvarez/e/B0107LJQEM

Facebook Author Page: https://www.facebook.com/AlexisAlvarezAuthor/

Goodreads: https://www.goodreads.com/author/show/14127116.Alexis_Alvarez

Twitter: https://twitter.com/AlexisAlvarezWr

Instagram: https://www.instagram.com/alexis_alvarez_writer/

Excerpt from Conquered by the Alien Prince

By Rebel West

"What you deserve," he snaps, his eyes wicked, "is a hard spanking right now for your continued insubordination. You take that, and maybe I'll consider rewarding you."

He's hard under my body, and I know that this time he won't be able to stop, no matter how many meetings he has.

"Do it," I whisper into his ear, and bite the lobe, hard.

He growls and presses his hands against my body. "You don't know what you're asking."

"Yes, I do. I want it."

"You really do?" He pulls back to look into my eyes.

I stick up my chin. "Are you afraid of me?"

He laughs, a dark, dirty chuckle. "Far from it, Cali. But once I start, you might be the one who experiences a little frisson of fear. You think you can handle that?"

"Yeah. I do." My voice is tough, confident.

He smiles, and suddenly my stomach flips. I'm prey, and he's the hunter. And I fucking love it. He scoops me up and puts me on my feet, in front of him. "Let's see you ask for it, then. Last time you disobeyed me, do you remember what I threatened?" He raises an eyebrow and touches his belt.

My whole body sparks, like I touched a live wire. "You told me... you'd use the punishment strap on me, if you needed to spank me again." My nipples are hard with desire.

"And here we are," he says conversationally. "And I do need to spank you again. So unfortunately for you," he slaps his thigh meaningfully, raising one eyebrow, "and your tender ass, this punishment is going to be far more memorable than the last one."

He unbelts something from around his waist. It looks like leather, and it's a lustrous black. Supple. My breath catches in my throat with fear and desire. The mixture is a drug to my veins.

He doubles it up and slaps it into his palm. "But we'll start with my hand, like last time. Come."

He nods at me and points to the spot between his spread legs.

I swallow hard and walk back to him, stand in between his thighs, feel the warmth of his body.

"Remove your garment, like last time." His voice is granite, and I wonder if it's taking all his willpower to play with me like this first, instead of just toss me onto the bed and fuck me hard.

Fumbling, I undo my jeans and slide them down my legs, and then off. I hold the denim in my hands until he takes it from me and tosses it behind him on the bed.

"This time we'll start without the panties," he says softly. "Give them to me, please." He holds out one hand.

When I hesitate, he snaps and points at my crotch, and I flush hard, then slide the panties down and step out of them. These he tucks into a pocket in his pants, and the sight of this is erotic enough to make my nipples harden and a surge of moisture flow between my thighs.

"Assume the position, Cali," he says, patting his lap. "We'll start this way at least, to warm you up for the strap. And as a reminder, you are to call me Master while I am disciplining you."

I slide over his lap, sucking in a breath as his strong, warm hands grab and reposition me.

"Thighs as wide as you can, please."

"Yes, Master." I do it, barely able to handle the suspense. My whole body is aching for his touch, rough, soft, all of it. I want it all.

"Good." I sense him raising his hand.

"Hold on!" I grab his leg. "Just a minute. Please."

"What?" He stills his movements.

"I'm—will it hurt more than last time?" I gulp, unsure about the strap.

"It will." He lays one hand on my buttocks and rubs. "Still no more than you can handle, but it will be worse than last time. You will tolerate it, even if you don't like it." He bends down to whisper, "After all, don't you deserve to be punished for your transgressions?"

Why does this shoot flares of arousal through my body?

"Yes," I answer, my skin on fire. "I do."

"Relax your buttocks. You know my rules." He taps my ass.

I force myself to soften my muscles.

"Your bottom is so soft," he remarks, stroking my skin. "It will be a pleasure to punish you and turn it red." Without warning, he lands a hard slap across my left ass cheek.

"Ouch." Before the word is fully out, he spanks me again on the other ass cheek, and begins a firm, punishing rhythm. He spanks harder than he started last time, and before long I am kicking up my feet and twisting on his lap.

"Stop moving," he warns, directing a volley of spanks at my sit spots, "or I'll do this." The spanks increase in intensity and then he slaps the base of my thighs until I cry out, "I'm sorry! I'll stop."

"See that you do," he tells me, and returns to the original pattern of spanking all over my ass.

It's hard not to wriggle and squirm, because my ass is already burning beyond belief, and the sting is making me want him so badly I could almost come right across his thighs, lying here, without even a touch to my clit. "Are you almost done?" I whimper.

He pushes my thighs apart and slaps his hand right onto my pussy. "I'll tell you when I'm done. Don't ask again. Your job is to take what I give. If you ask again, I'll spank here." He slaps again, harder, against my soft nether lips, and I almost fly apart.

"Lock," I beg. "Master," and I don't know what I'm asking: *Stop, more, please?*

"Shush," he commands. "Lie still and accept your punishment. We still have quite a ways to go."

* * *

Conquered by the Alien Prince by Rebel West
<u>Amazon and KU</u>

Conquered by the Alien Prince - Sample

Conquered by the Alien Prince
Luminar Masters, Book 1
An Alien Sci-Fi Romance
By Rebel West

A sexy silver alien with ripped abs, a top-secret patient with a mystery illness, and unicorns – and Dr. Emily Taylor's experience on Luminar is just getting started!

It's not easy being one of Earth's top neuroscientists at age twenty-four, but Emily's dedicated her life to research, leaving little time for dating. When she travels on a confidential mission to Luminar, her local delegation lead – handsome Prince Lock, turns out to be domineering in all the right ways to bring out her passion.

But he's an alien prince and she's an earth human, and there's no way they could have a *real* relationship. Plus, anti-human protestors and threats against the Luminar monarchy are causing havoc, putting her mission, and maybe even her life, into jeopardy.

This interplanetary romance will need to have a bond of steel, because the glorious nights of kinky passion are just the start to an everlasting HEA.

Enjoy the first book in the Luminar Masters Series by Rebel West. The books are interconnected and can be read in any order. Guaranteed HEA and no cheating!

Note: This book contains elements of dominance and submission. If this material offends you, please do not buy this book.